A Prescription for Beauty

A Dose of Love, Book 3
By
Jill Boyce

ISBN: 978-1-0880-5806-0

Acknowledgments

I praise God, who whispered these stories to my heart and placed the perfect people along my writing path at the right time.

I thank my husband, children, father, in-laws, stepmother, family, and friends for their love and support. I'm especially thankful that my husband and mother-in-law read my drafts multiple times and give honest, yet loving, feedback.

I am grateful to my mentor and friend, Carrie Turansky, for her generous spirit and wisdom, and my publisher and editor, Cynthia Hickey, for believing in my work.

I give thanks for my mother, who passed away six years ago on the day of my daughter's birth. Her death inspired my first book, *Harte Broken*. She instilled in me the love of books and the desire to dream big. I love you, Mom.

My hope is my stories will provide comfort, laughter, and encouragement to my readers. May God bless you all.

1 Samuel 16:7: But the LORD said to Samuel, "Do not consider his appearance or his height, for I have rejected him. The LORD does not look at the things people look at. People look at the outward appearance, but the LORD looks at the heart."

.

Chapter 1

December 11, 2019, Wednesday

Marley Bakersfield leaned forward, peering at her reflection closer in the mirror. She brushed her bangs behind her ear, willing them to stay put. *Hmm. She could still see it.* Pulling a small silver compact out of her leather bag sitting on the bench behind her, she opened it and retrieved the white sponge on the top. Pressing it into the light-colored makeup, she dabbed the creamy camouflage across her forehead, begging it to cover the scar. *There.* Not perfect, but now the imperfection lay hidden underneath layers of makeup and her side-swept crimson bangs.

Clicking the compact closed, Marley gazed at her image once more. Although everything appeared intact, her emerald green eyes flashed a hint of doubt.

Tara Madding, Marley's best friend and sole confidant since the anatomy lab incident of 2006, entered the locker room. The pair had met while commiserating over meticulously dissecting an essential nerve branch, only to accidentally snip it the next day. This error resulted in the two of them staying at the lab until past midnight to reconnect the nerves using skills they had both yet to learn. Although traumatic at the time, the experience left them with a complete anatomy project and a treasured friendship.

Tara smacked her pink bubblegum and blew a giant orb. It popped, and she sent her friend a grin. "Are you reapplying makeup again? It's not noticeable. At all."

Marley shook her head and slipped the compact bag into her bag. "I only did a touch-up. And it is noticeable. It's been noticeable my whole life. You don't understand. Not all of us have flawless skin and perfect figures despite consuming a mountain of snack cakes for breakfast." She pointed her gaze at the plastic-wrapped sponge cake in her friend's hand. It was maddening. Marley loved her friend, but with the metabolism of a hummingbird, Tara could eat anything and never gain an ounce. On the other hand, Marley had to live off black coffee and long jogs to stay in shape. Life could be unfair.

"I don't know why you are so hard on yourself. You're gorgeous. Everyone would kill for your long, wavy red hair and green eyes. And that skin. It's the perfect blend of peaches and cream. And it's not like you're not in killer shape, too." Tara arched a brow to make her point.

Marley shrugged. Tara would never totally understand. A memory from Marley's childhood flickered through her mind. She stood outside her suburban house, the brand-new bike she'd received as a birthday gift from her parents by her side. It was pink, shiny, and had a multi-colored of plastic tassels on the ends of the handlebars. She'd beamed as she walked it down the sidewalk to show it to the neighborhood kids. She'd just learned how to ride a bike and couldn't wait to take her new one for a test drive.

"Marley, is that a new bike?" A chestnut-haired boy named Charlie adjusted the brim of his worn, navy baseball hat and inspected her gift closer. "It looks girly. I bet it doesn't go fast."

Charlie had tortured her since kindergarten. He often worked in conjunction with Stacey Blackstone. Marley looked around for his co-conspirator but did not find her. Marley furrowed her brow. "Well, it looks girly because I'm a girl. It's supposed to look this way. And it does, too, go fast."

He cocked his head to the side and tossed her a challenging smirk. "Well, then let's see it. Let's see what you've got."

A second voice, smooth as silk, interrupted them, "Yeah, Marley. Let's see how fast your new bike can go. I bet you can't beat me. My daddy got me this bike, and it's the best one on the market. Daddy says so."

2

Marley spun around, and her eyes landed upon her arch-nemesis. *Ugh. She. Was. The. Worst.* Marley knew from Sunday school she should love her neighbors and all that kindness stuff, but Stacey had to be the exception to the rule. "Stacey," she said it more as a statement of fact than a greeting.

Stacey's aqua eyes taunted her. "Marley. Come on. What do you say? You and me. Let's have a race. The first one to pass old Mr. Bennington's house wins." She nudged the kickstand on her bike and pulled it alongside her.

A small crowd of kids had gathered around as this interchange took place, and now Marley had an audience. Swallowing hard, Marley knew her bike-riding skills lacked. She'd only mastered the ability to balance for more than ten or twenty feet within the last week. Scanning the group, her eyes darted to Benjamin Miller's kind gaze. She'd had a crush on him since preschool but didn't dare divulge this information. She couldn't back down now.

Marley punted her kickstand out of the way and gripped both handlebars tighter. She narrowed her eyes and stared at Stacey. "You're on."

"Careful, there, Marley. I don't know if that bike will hold your weight." Snickers came from the peanut gallery.

Marley's neck burned, and her cheeks warmed. She'd always carried a comfortable cushion around her midsection. Since her mother fell in love with television baking shows, their house produced more loaves and cakes than Miller's Bakery. As a consequence, over third grade, Marley had picked up at least an additional ten pounds. That, combined with her frizzy, red ringlets, made her self-conscious. And Stacey knew it. "It will hold my weight fine." She glared at her perfect, blond adversary. Swinging one leg over her bike and resting the other one on the ground, Marley sucked in a deep breath.

Charlie gave the countdown, "On your mark, get set.... go!"

Marley shot ahead, pumping her legs with fury, determined not to let Stacey win. After several feet, she pulled ahead to take the lead. With Mr. Bennington's house in sight, Marley thought she had won. Blinded by hope and vindication, she didn't see the sizeable rock on the road before her. Marley's front tire caught on it and sent her flying over the handlebars. She whizzed through the air and landed with a thud, scraping her forehead and scalp across the concrete road below.

Pain seared her mind, and Marley's head throbbed. Footsteps came running behind her. She rolled over on one side, lifting a hand to her head. She groaned, "Ow!"

A hand reached out to her. "Marley, are you okay?"

Lifting her eyes, she saw Benjamin. Marley accepted his hand, both embarrassed and grateful. "Thanks. My head hurts pretty bad. I need to go home and get cleaned up. My father's going to be so mad about the bike. It was brand new."

"You want me to walk you home? I can come back and get your bike for you, too." Benjamin raised his forehead.

A warm flush of appreciation spread through her heart. "That would be—"

Stacey cut off Marley's response, "Oh, Benjamin, she doesn't need your help. It's barely a scrape. I told you, Marley, you couldn't beat my bike. Look what happened when you tried. You really should be more careful."

Charlie piped in, "I guess we were right. You crushed your bike, Marley." He tilted his head and sneered.

Hot tears sprang to her eyes, and Marley refused to let the other kids see her cry. She dropped Benjamin's hand and sprinted toward her house.

Once home, her father gave her a long speech about personal responsibility and taking care of things. Though a surgeon, her father had spent twenty years in the army, and it took a lot to rattle him. Her mother demonstrated more empathy, helping Marley wash debris and dirt off her forehead. She applied some ointment, a bandage, and offered another round of muffins leftover from breakfast that morning. That was her answer to everything; eat something.

The next day, Marley begged her mother to let her stay home-- out of character for Marley. She made top grades and, most years, had perfect attendance. Her mother insisted that a scrape did not constitute a week off school and a doctor's note from her father, so she shipped Marley onto the school bus and waved goodbye.

As Marley stepped onto the bus, the first words out of Stacey's mouth were, "Oh, look, it's Marley." Stacey peered at Marley's bandaged forehead. She spoke without sincerity, "Marley, I felt bad about your wreck yesterday. You're probably going to have a scar." A look of inspiration crossed Stacey's face. "Maybe we can call you Scarly Marley."

It took about 2.5 seconds for the other kids on the bus to start chanting Scarly Marley over and over again.

Marley tucked her head down and tried to pull her hair across her forehead to hide the bandage. She marched to the back of the bus, huddling into an empty seat. Trying to shield her wound and tears from the brutal crowd at the front, Marley draped her hands over her head.

The sound of another bubble popping rocked Marley out of the painful memory and into the present. She stared at her face once more in the locker room mirror of Preston-Smith Memorial Hospital in D.C., and all she could think about were those words. *Scarly Marley.* Despite all the work she'd done to overcome her past, that chant still haunted her--*Scarly Marley.*

Tara's eyes narrowed, and she planted her hands on her hips. "Did you hear me?"

"Huh? I'm sorry. I zoned out for a minute. What did you say?"

"I said, you know the saying…beauty is only skin deep, right? Besides, you're gorgeous. And more importantly, you have a great heart. I don't think anyone else in this hospital has gone on as many medical mission trips as you. Or worked as many overtime call hours for free." Her friend smacked her gum again and bent down to retie the neon pink laces on her glittered sneakers. Being the hospital's best pediatrician, Tara could get away with wearing fun shoes and loud-colored scrubs. Her occupation almost demanded it.

Marley glanced at her own starched, cornflower blue scrubs, pressed white coat, and rubber clogs. She dressed like everyone else in her department. She looked like she was supposed to look. And that was always Marley's goal. *Blend in. Fit in.*

"Yeah, right. Skin deep. I hear you." She appeased her friend, but Marley knew the truth. No matter how much she tried to change her exterior, inside, she felt like that tormented little girl. Inside she still felt like chubby Scarly Marley. And she didn't know if that would ever change.

Chapter 2

December 11, 2019, Wednesday

Marley changed and exited the locker room dressed in skinny black pants, black patent heels, and an eggplant button-up dress shirt underneath her starched white lab coat.

Tara had grabbed Marley's arm as she pushed open the locker room door, ready to go to her meeting. "Hey, can you swing by and do a quick consult on a patient? She came in early this morning after she burned her arm on the kitchen stove door. The ER dressed it with ointment and a nonstick bandage, but I'd feel better if you took a look. The burn doesn't look too deep, but still, you're the expert."

Marley pushed through the door and swung her bag over her shoulder. She turned around, holding the door open for her friend. "Sure, no problem. I still have about an hour until my meeting, so that should be plenty of time to take a look and make recommendations. Besides, the children's floor is my favorite spot in the hospital. The last time I went up there, I ran into a staff member making balloon animals."

Tara sent her friend a grin. "Thanks, Marley. I appreciate it, and I know her parents will too. They felt terrible about the accident, and her mom has not left her side since she arrived. If nothing else, I think your presence will offer reassurance."

Marley nodded and turned to go see her last patient of the day.
"Oh, and Marley…"
Spinning around, she met Tara's encouraging eyes. "Yeah?"

Tara's grin widened. "I'll be praying for your meeting to go well. I know how important it is for you to make partner in the practice."

Partner. It had been the sole focus of Marley's to make partner in her prestigious plastic surgery practice since she signed her contract years ago. And now, it seemed like her dream might come true. She might make partner in the Fortwright, Sloan, and Thomas Surgery Group, Inc. Perhaps if her life appeared perfect on the outside, then she'd feel good enough on the inside. "Thanks. I'll take all the prayers I can get."

Tucking her bangs behind her ear again, Marley ensured the external reminder from her past remained hidden. She took hurried steps down the white-tiled hallway, and the scent of bleach intermixed with peppermint cocoa filled the air.

This time of year, the children's floor of the hospital tried to bring cheer and happiness to an otherwise daunting place for its temporary residents. Strands of homemade garland created from red and green construction paper in the shape of stars and trees lined the hallway. A silver Christmas tree adorned with neon pink and purple ornaments boasted hope and festivity at the end of the hall. Underneath its branches sat various sized packages wrapped in bright colors and large bows. Marley hated to imagine what spending Christmas in the hospital must be like for these children. It brought a smile to her face to see the staff's attempt to make the holiday special.

Arriving at Tara's patient's door, Marley paused. Her eyes fell upon the beautiful family inside.

A middle-aged man stood at the foot of the bed, pacing back and forth, while a blond woman devoid of makeup, wearing a worried frown, stood at the head of the bed. She patted the young girl's forehead, who laid in the bed with at least three blankets covering her.

Marley knew the girl to be five years old from the brief report Tara had given her. She had springy, blond curls and glittering blue eyes. White gauze and tape encased her right forearm. Still, despite her injury, the little girl broke through her parents' concerned tension with a buoyant giggle.

Rapping on the open door, Marley announced her arrival, "Knock, knock. May I come in?" She gave the patient a smile and waited.

The mother raised her head, and her hand paused from its task of stroking the child's hair. "Oh, you must be the plastic surgeon. The other doctor who was here earlier said you might stop by. Come in, come in."

Taking a few slow steps toward the patient, Marley paused at the sanitizing station and cleaned her hands before scooting next to the little girl. "Hi, my name is Dr. Marley. What's your name?" Marley raised her brow, waiting for a response.

The little girl grinned, revealing a gap-toothed smile that melted Marley's heart. "My name's Emma, and I'm five." She raised a hand showing all five fingers for emphasis.

"Wow, Emma, you're a big girl, then. I heard you got hurt on your stove at home. Is that right?"

The girl bobbed her head but remained silent.

"Can you tell me how it happened?" Marley pulled a chair over and took a seat so she could get closer to the little girl.

The girl's eyes darted to her mother for a second.

Her mom nodded her head.

Emma shifted her gaze back to Marley and jumped into her story, "Well, my momma and I were making cookies. I love cookies. Cookies are my favorite food. I like chocolate chip cookies, ginger cookies, sugar cookies—"

Emma's mother placed a gentle hand on her daughter's shoulder. "Emma, dear, I don't think the nice doctor needs to hear about all the cookies you like. Can you tell her what happened to your arm?"

The little girl frowned at the interruption but redirected her story. "Fine. So, we were making cookies, and I told my mom I could help get them out. She tried to stop me." Emma looked at her mother, accusation in her eyes. "And I could have done it, but the tray was heavy."

Emma's mother squeezed her daughter's shoulder, and her brow crinkled. "I feel terrible. Just awful. I told her not to get near the stove, but she is so fast. I stepped over to grab the oven mitt out of a drawer, and by the time I turned around, she'd already opened the door and burned her arm. I'm the worst mother ever." Tears pooled behind the mother's eyes.

Marley shook her head. "I assure you this happens more often than you might think. And you are not the worst mother ever." Marley turned her attention to the girl again. "Emma, would it be okay if I took a look at your arm? Just to make sure, I don't need to give you a cooler bandage. Maybe something pink?"

With her eyes lighting up at the word "pink," Emma jutted her arm forward for the examination.

"Thanks, Emma. I promise to be quick, and I'll try not to hurt you. Okay?"

Emma nodded. "Okay."

Fifteen minutes later, Marley completed her exam and redressed the site with a fresh layer of ointment. She covered it with a nonadherent gauze and a fuchsia cling wrap, securing it with paper tape. "There, that should do it. Do you have any questions, Emma?"

The little girl raised her eyes to Marley and stared for a few seconds as if considering what to ask her doctor. "Do you like cookies? Because my mommy brought some we made earlier. You can have one if you want." She pulled out a plastic baggie filled with chocolate chip cookies and shoved it in Marley's face.

The scent of butter and sugar wafted below Marley's nose. It brought with it memories of her childhood and her mother's baking. A fragrance that should embody love and warmth left only a pit in Marley's stomach. She recalled her mother forcing baked goods upon her and being teased by the neighbor kids for being chubby. She smiled at the gesture, not having the heart to tell the kid she didn't eat sweets. "Thank you, Emma. I bet you did a great job." Taking the baggie from the little girl's hand, Marley tucked it away in her white coat pocket.

Emma's father stepped forward. "Now, honey, let's give the doctor a chance to see her other patients. I bet she's got a lot of people to take care of today. Thank you, Dr. Marley, for treating our little girl so well." He sent Marley a grateful smile.

Emma's mother bobbed her head in agreement. "Yes, thank you. I forgot to ask if you think the burn will leave a scar?"

Marley felt the blood drain from her face. It was a valid question. *Would it scar?* She didn't know why it bothered her to hear those words aloud still. Shaking her head slowly, Marley replied, "I don't think so. We won't know for certain for several more months, but I believe it will do well if you follow my instructions. So, no, I'm hoping for no scar." Marley stood, waved goodbye to the kind family, and exited the room.

As Marley walked down the hallway, leaving the children's floor behind, she glanced at her watch, noting the time. *4:50 p.m.* She didn't want to be late for her meeting. She picked up her pace and rushed ahead toward what she hoped would be her perfect future. The perfect job, the perfect home, the perfect life. Maybe if she willed it, then she'd start to feel perfect on the inside, too. Maybe.

~

Arriving at the plastic surgery practice conference room, Marley took her seat at exactly 4:59 p.m.

Within a few minutes, Dr. Fortwright and Dr. Thomas walked in and joined her at the table.

She shared cordial greetings with her two of her soon-to-be partners. After shaking their hands, she placed hers back in her lap, clasping them tightly. As the minutes ticked by waiting for the group's final member, Dr. Sloan, to make an appearance, Marley picked at her fingernails.

Ten minutes later, wearing a self-assured grin and an excess of product in his dark brown hair, strolled in Dr. Jesse Sloan. As part of the practice, although not yet a partner, Marley worked with Dr. Sloan regularly.

They'd shared consults on cases and conversed at the coffee machine in the office countless times. She always sensed he wanted more than a work relationship, though. And with her focus on her career and making partner, she'd tried to avoid his advances. *For the most part.*

She couldn't deny his good looks. In fact, most of the female population cast furtive glances his way and shared whispered giggles when he passed through the hospital's halls. And he knew it.

He nodded her way. "Dr. Bakersfield."

"Dr. Sloan." She tossed him a quick nod and then resumed shuffling through the papers in front of her.

The other two partners of the practice gave Dr. Sloan a good ribbing at his lack of punctuality. "Did you get lost, son?" Dr. Fortwright chuckled.

Dr. Thomas leaned back in his chair and crossed his arms in front of his chest. The salt and peppered hair at his temples added a measure of wisdom. He looked as if he'd been practicing medicine all his life. "We thought we'd have to send a search party out looking for you." His tanned face broke into a wide grin, and the three men chortled.

Waving his hand, Dr. Sloan brushed aside his partner's jovial rebukes. "Nah. I got hung up at the hospital. One of the new nurses needed my help on a case."

Marley bet she did. *Probably the case of the missing Friday night date.* She wondered if Jesse had cracked the code for the new nurse. At this thought, Marley couldn't hide her amusement.

Jesse had taken his seat and turned his attention to Marley. "What's so funny?"

Marley forced her lips to draw into a straight line and tried to become serious. After all, her chance at partnership was on the line. "Oh, nothing. I was thinking about a case from earlier today. That's all." Her eyes flitted toward Dr. Thomas. "Should we get started?"

Picking up the papers on the table before him, Dr. Thomas tapped them to straighten them out before returning the pile to the table. "Yes, by all means. So, Dr. Bakersfield, you've worked at our practice now for a while. And I think I speak for the other gentleman here today when I say we couldn't be more pleased with your work ethic and medical expertise."

Her cheeks burned at the compliment. Marley sent him a smile. "Thank you. I'm glad to hear it. I've enjoyed working with you. I love my job."

Clearing his throat, Dr. Fortwright jumped in, "And we understand that you wish to be considered for a role as a partner in the medical practice, is that correct?"

Nodding her head, Marley confirmed his assertion, "Yes, absolutely. It would be an honor to become a full partner."

Dr. Fortwright leaned forward, placing his elbows on the table. He rested his chin on his fingertips, steepled together, and gave her an even stare. "Good, glad to hear it. I believe I speak for the group when I say you would be an excellent fit for our practice's leadership. Of course, you know with partnership comes more responsibilities as well as rewards."

Her palms sweating, Marley wiped them discreetly on her pants under the table. "I would expect nothing less."

"Great. Dr. Sloan, Dr. Fortwright, and I will meet after the Christmas holiday to make a final choice and let you know. It is a big decision. We haven't considered anyone for partner in a few years. We don't take any of this lightly." Dr. Thomas shot his eyes toward his youngest partner. "Dr. Sloan, do you have anything to add? Or any other questions for Dr. Bakersfield?"

A smile threatened to tug up the corners of Jesse's lips, but he retained his smooth demeanor. "Actually, I have several more questions for her. Our paths cross in the hospital, but with everyone's busy schedule, we rarely have time to talk." He swiveled in his seat and locked his chocolate brown eyes on hers. "So, what do you say? We could continue this conversation as a working dinner." He glanced at his shiny gold watch on his wrist. "It's only 5:45 p.m. The perfect time to grab a reservation."

Dr. Fortwright clapped his hands together. "Perfect idea! I'd join you both, but my wife threatened to leave me if I came home tonight a minute past 6:30 p.m., so I need to go." He rose from his seat and collected his papers as if the matter had been settled.

Sliding his own stack of forms into a brown briefcase, Dr. Thomas shook his head. "I can't offer my company tonight either, I'm afraid. My daughter has a ballet recital, and I've missed the last two. But I agree, you two should go. It would be a great opportunity for Dr. Bakersfield to learn more about the inner workings of the practice. We can all reconvene after the holidays to finalize things. Of course, if Dr. Sloan can't answer any questions you may have tonight, please reach out to us as well."

The two older gentlemen shook her hand and left the room.

Still seated in her chair, Marley hesitated to raise her eyes to Dr. Sloan's. She wouldn't deny his good looks, but something about him gave her pause. Perhaps it because Marley didn't want anything to derail her career plans. Or maybe it was the fact that since middle school, she'd never considered that a boy, or in this case, a man, might actually like her. Whatever the source of her hesitation, Marley didn't know if sharing a meal with him demonstrated wisdom on multiple levels. She didn't want to give him the wrong idea.

"So, ready for dinner?"

His voice breaking the silent tension startled her. "Uh, well, you know Dr. Sloan, if you're busy and it's not a good night for it, we can always schedule something for after Christmas. Maybe with all the partners?"

He rose and took a few steps toward her, closing the space between them. "Jesse. Please call me Jesse."

"Uh, okay. Right. Jesse."

"So, dinner?" He raised a brow and waited for her response.

Her neck burned. She couldn't help but feel silly. *This would be a simple work function—a meal. They would eat, drink, discuss the partnership, and then go home. Nothing too scandalous. Right?* She gave him a small nod of the head. "Okay. Dinner." *Just dinner.* She rose from her seat and followed him out of the conference room and into the night, praying she wasn't making a huge mistake.

Chapter 3

December 11, 2019, Wednesday

Marley sat through her dinner with Dr. Jesse Sloan, making chit-chat and discussing her future at the surgical practice. Every time he drove the conversation into personal territory by complimenting her eyes or sending her a flirtatious grin, Marley steered the discussion back to the highway of professionalism. Or at least she tried.

Sighing, Marley exited the restaurant and thanked Jesse for his time and the meal. She shook his hand and spun on her heel, hurrying to her car before he could suggest extending the evening or worse—kiss her. It wasn't that she'd had a bad time. He was gorgeous; she couldn't dispute that fact. And a charmer. But she didn't see herself saying the words, "'til death do us part," to him any time soon, and she didn't need any distractions right now.

Sliding into her black hatchback, Marley slammed the door and shoved her key into the ignition. She navigated the thick traffic around the beltway, her hands gripping the steering wheel tight. Marley loved everything about the city except for driving in the fast-paced traffic. One wrong move and the car behind her would smash her flat.

When she pulled off the exit to her house, Marley exhaled a long sigh she'd been holding for the duration of the drive home. *What a day.* Reflecting on the day's events, she couldn't believe she'd survived dinner with Jesse unscathed. Working with him as a partner might prove a challenge, but she'd dealt with worse scenarios throughout medical school. She felt confident she could manage him.

A ringing from within her purse snapped Marley out of her thoughts. She hit the phone button on her steering wheel, accepting the call. "Hello?"

"Marley? Marley? Can you hear me?" her mother's concerned voice shouted across Marley's stereo.

Marley stretched her arm to the volume knob and turned it down before answering, "Mom? Is that you?"

"Yes, dear, it's me. I hate to bother you…but there's been an accident."

Heading down the street leading to her townhouse, Marley picked up her pace. "An accident? What kind of accident?" She pulled into her driveway and stopped the car. Turning the car off, she threw open the door and grabbed her bag. Marley stepped out and turned the call over to her phone's receiver. "Mom? Are you still there?"

"…And I don't know how in the world it happened, but there you have it. So, can you do it?"

"Sorry, Mom, I missed a lot of what you said when I got out of the car. Can I do what?" Marley wedged the phone between her ear and shoulder as she walked up the stairs to her front door.

"I said, can you come home and take over the practice for a little while? Maybe six weeks or so? It might not take that long, but you never know—"

Marley cut off her mother's monologue, "Wait, take over what practice, Mom? I don't understand. Can you start over?"

"Marley, are you listening to me? You never listen to me. I told you that your father fell off a ladder and broke his leg. He's in a cast of some sort, and his doctor told me he couldn't work for at least six weeks. Maybe longer. The good news is he didn't hit his head. It's a miracle he didn't kill himself."

"Dad fell off a ladder. Doing what?" Marley shoved her key into the front door lock and turned it. Pushing the door open, she stepped inside. Marley and her parents had a complicated relationship. While her mother had the perfect wife, mother, and homemaker thing down, she also had a penchant for being subtly critical at times. And Marley's father…well…he'd finished his time with the military as a colonel in the army. With experience in combat surgery, he could be intimidating, too.

"He was cleaning the gutters. I told him to hire someone to do it, but you know your father. Completely bull-headed. So, he has to rest and let his leg heal. He needs someone to cover his general surgery practice. He said there is no way he can be gone that long. He thinks Blackstone Haven Hospital is trying to force him out anyway, but he's always been a little paranoid. I promised I'd call to see if you could take a short leave of absence and come here to cover the practice for him."

Marley's jaw fell. Her father had put a lot of expectations on her plate before, but this...this topped them all. "Mom...I don't know if I can take that long away from my job."

"Well, you know Christmas is right around the corner. It's perfect timing, really, if you think about it. We never get you home for more than a day or two, and this way, we could all soak up the holiday."

"I know, Mom, but I'll have to ask my practice if I can get that much time off...and I'm up for partner. I don't know what they'll think about me taking a long leave."

Her mother cleared her throat.

Oh no. Here comes the major guilt trip. Probably a monologue about duty would follow. It wasn't that Marley didn't love her parents or want to help them, but her childhood and the town of Blackstone Haven harbored painful memories for Marley. She didn't relish the idea of returning to her hometown.

"Besides, when was the last time you came for a visit? Hmm?"

Marley shuffled her feet and stared at the wood floor. "Oh, I don't know."

Her mother clicked her tongue. "Well, I do. Five months ago, you came home for your father's birthday. You stayed for one day and night, and the next morning you shot out of here like the place had burst into flames. It's about time you made a trip home, one where you unpack your bag and stay awhile."

Marley stalled, pacing up and down the narrow hallway leading from her living room to the kitchen in her townhouse. "Well..."

"You know, your father and I aren't getting younger. This may be the last Christmas we get to spend together. You never know."

Oh great. Sally Bakersfield had gone full press. She'd reached into the depths of her guilt artillery and pulled out the big guns. Marley knew she'd lost the battle. And she did feel bad for her father. Although she didn't understand why he didn't hang up the practice, retire, and take it easy. Letting that thought marinate in her mind for a second, Marley chuckled.

"What's funny? Nothing about this is funny?" Her mother's voice sounded unusually stern.

Composing herself, Marley became serious again. "No, it's not that. I'm not laughing at dad's accident. I was envisioning him retired. The image of him sitting in a chair on a beach somewhere with a fruity drink in hand made me giggle."

Her mother let out a snort. "No, no chance of that happening. You know your father. He said, 'This town needs me. My patients need me.' I figure he'll drop over at his desk or while walking the hospital's corridors one day. Believe me, I tried to talk him into selling the practice, but he won't hear of it."

"No, I can't imagine Dad handing over anything of his to someone else, much less the practice he built from the ground up."

"Plus, there are a lot of people in this community he treats for free or at a reduced rate. If he left, he fears they wouldn't have access to care." Her mother's voice softened, "I know you two have had your differences. Sometimes even you and I don't see things the same way, but your father is a good man. He means well."

Silence hung in the air as neither of the women spoke for several seconds.

Marley released a quiet sigh. She'd have to do it. She didn't know how or what her future partners might say, but Marley didn't see that she had a choice in the matter. *Duty calls.* She'd have to answer. "Okay, Mom. I'll call my office tomorrow morning and ask for a leave of absence. A short leave." Marley emphasized the word short.

"Oh, thank you, Honeybun. You don't know what a blessing you will be to us. Your father will be so relieved. I'm heading to the hospital again this evening. I dropped by the house to grab him a few things, but I can't wait to tell him the news."

"Don't get too excited, Mom. I'll have to call the Blackstone Haven Hospital and see about getting privileges. I haven't practiced general surgery in years."

"Well, I'm sure that won't be too difficult. You kept up your board certification, right?"

"I did. But still, if the hospital doesn't approve me to work there and treat patients, I can't do anything about that. I'm a plastic surgeon, you know." Her father had overlooked her desire to enter plastic surgery most of her adult life. She suspected he'd hoped she might pursue general surgery and join him at his practice one day.

Marley's mother spoke with hurried excitement, "That's fine, dear. You call and get yourself packed. Oh, I can't wait to see you! I'll start baking later tonight. As soon as I get home from the hospital."

Marley stopped pacing and cast her eyes around her clean stainless-steel kitchen devoid of any evidence of food preparation. "Mom, you know I don't eat sugar. Please don't make a bunch of stuff. And I'm vegan--I don't eat eggs, dairy, and definitely not meat."

"Pshaw. No sugar. Whoever heard of such a thing? And vegan? When did that happen?"

"I started cutting animal products out of my diet over the summer. You'd be amazed how much better it makes the body feel. I upped my long-distance runs in a matter of weeks. And my joints don't ache like they used to when I ate meat. All that stuff fuels inflammation in the body."

"Oh, I know what I'll do. I'll grab you some organic eggs and chicken. I think Blackstone Farm sells fresh eggs at their weekly market. Let me add that to my to-do list."

"Mom, organic eggs are still eggs—"

Her mother cut her off, "I hate to run, Honeybun, but I've got to go. Your father's going to think I abandoned him if I don't get back soon. Call me tomorrow and let me know what time you'll arrive. Love you." Her mother's voice disappeared.

Marley stared at the home screen on her phone and shook her head. "Bye, Mom." She prayed her future medical partners would understand about her family emergency. Hopefully, her time away wouldn't last longer than a few weeks. Perhaps, she could convince her father to sell his practice. Then, he and her mother could enjoy time together, and she could get back to her goal of making partner at Fortwright, Sloan, and Thomas Surgery Group, Inc.--far away from the painful past in Blackstone Haven.

Marley had no doubt that a mountain of sugary baked goods awaited her at her childhood home. And none of them would be vegan.

Chapter 4

December 12, 2019, Thursday

Marley rushed through the hospital's lobby and jumped on the open elevator. She headed upstairs to the locker room to change into scrubs and face the task at the top of her to-do list— calling her future partners about her upcoming leave. Drawing in a deep breath, Marley held it for a few seconds before releasing it. She prayed they'd understand her situation.

After dressing in the locker room, Marley pulled out her phone and punched in the number to the practice's most senior partner, Dr. Fortwright. She gulped as it rang.

"Dr. Fortwright speaking," his serious voice bellowed through the line.

"Yes, hello, Dr. Fortwright. This is Dr. Marley Bakersfield."

"Oh, Dr. Bakersfield, to what do I owe the pleasure of this early morning call?"

"Well…I hate to ask this, especially with our most recent discussion in consideration, but my father had a fall."

"I hate to hear that. He's not hurt badly, I hope?"

Marley glanced around the empty locker room and shifted her weight. "Um, no. I mean, yes. He was hurt, but I believe he'll be okay."

"Well, that's good to hear, but I'm not sure how it relates to me?"

"That's the thing, Dr. Fortwright. It does relate to you, and me, too, actually, because when my father fell, he broke his leg. He's a physician, and my mother says he can't work for several weeks at least. She called me last night to ask for my help, and I hoped you might give me a leave of absence."

Silence answered her.

"Just for a few weeks. My father is a military man and the toughest guy I know. I'm sure he'll be up sooner than the doctor expects, but he needs someone to take over his practice in the meantime. Temporarily. And he doesn't have a partner....so..."

"So, you'd like to take leave to go help your father?"

"Exactly. If it isn't too much to ask? I know our practice here is busy, but I hoped Dr. Sloan and some other physicians might bear some of the load for me? I promise to return as soon as possible."

"I suppose it's not an unreasonable request. You know we are considering your partnership, though. We need to be able to reach you in case we have any questions or if there is a case of yours that requires consultation or discussion."

A huge breath escaped her lips, and Marley's shoulders relaxed. "Absolutely! Of course. Any time. You have my number, but I'll call the secretary and leave it with her, too. And as I said before, I don't think it will take more than a few weeks. Four weeks, maybe six at the most?" She asked the question as much for herself as for the benefit of her boss.

"Six weeks? I surely hope not. We'd like to have you back by then if not before, to commence your partnership. Dr. Thomas told me last night he's thinking about cutting back his hours, and we'll need you to step in by then."

Marley nodded her head, though her boss couldn't see her. "I understand. I'll let you know a more definite timeframe once I get home. Thank you, sir, for understanding."

"No problem, Dr. Bakersfield. By the way, what type of medicine did you say your father practices?"

"Uh... it's general surgery. It's a small practice. My hometown isn't like D.C. It's more rural. Lots of farms, shops, tree-lined sidewalks. That sort of thing."

"So, you're going to be the town surgeon? Do they know you do plastic surgery now?"

This fact hadn't seemed to escape anyone, much less, Marley. "Yes, they know. I'm getting ready to call the hospital about privileges today, but I am dual-boarded in general and plastic surgery."

More silence.

"Uh, sir?"

"Yes, Dr. Bakersfield, was there something else. I have patients to see."

"Oh, yes, I do, too. I wanted to thank you. Again. Thanks."

"Not a problem. Keep us informed. Now I must go. Have a good day Dr. Bakersfield."

Marley turned off her phone and slid it into her bag. Straightening her shirt, she gave herself a quick glance in the mirror. The thought of returning home and running into people from her childhood sent a shiver up her spine. She shuddered. *A few weeks. That's all. It would only be for a few weeks. Marley squared her shoulders and stared at herself.* She was a successful surgeon now and not the chubby, frizzy-haired, third grader from years ago.

The light mark on her forehead, a few millimeters in width, peeked out from underneath her wavy bangs. If all those things held true, why did she still feel like ten-year-old Scarly Marley? Brushing her hand across her bangs, she arranged them, so they covered her scar and pulled her eyes away from her reflection. *A few weeks. It would be fine.* She hoped.

~

Marley hoped to bump into Tara before finishing her shift at the hospital Thursday morning. Sadly, the day became a blur, and Marley never had a chance to tell her best friend about the impending adventure. If she could call it that. It felt more like a sentence.

Marley needed Tara's help in getting things together for her trip. Blackstone Haven was no D.C. Several shops lined the town's main street, but there wasn't a makeup hub or designer coffee shop on every corner. Which reminded Marley; she needed to pick up good coffee grounds to take with her. She couldn't leave the quality of her daily caffeine infusion to chance.

As Marley stepped out of the hospital's double glass doors, she tried to imagine not setting foot in this place for the next six weeks. It had become a second home to her, and the nurses and staff often felt like family. And this family didn't know her past. They didn't know about her inadequacies, insecurities, and embarrassments. Marley liked it that way. *Keep the past in the past.* Throw on her armor of beauty--concealer for her scar and hair products to tame her wild mane. Some might call it a façade, but after enduring the torture of middle school and then high school in her small town, these armaments seemed vital. Necessary even.

Her phone rang, and Marley dug around in her purse for it. She recognized Tara's name on the screen and smiled. *Perfect timing.* She hit the green button. "Hey, I was going to call you. I have big news."

"Bigger than the news buzzing around the hospital that you are on the brink of becoming the youngest partner at the premier plastic surgery group in the metro area?"

Marley raised her brow even though her friend couldn't see her face. "What? The whole hospital knows?"

Tara responded, "Well, it's not really a secret, is it? Pretty exciting, huh?" She smacked what was undoubtedly gum in the background.

"You know that stuff is terrible for your teeth. It's full of sugar and empty calories, and you're going to get a cavity. You're a doctor—you should know better."

"Yes, Mom."

Marley could almost hear her friend rolling her eyes. "I'm serious. Get off the gum habit."

"Okay, okay, but didn't you say you had big news? If it's not about the partnership, then what is it?" Tara changed the subject.

"Right. I got a phone call from my mom yesterday. She told me my dad fell off a ladder and broke his leg."

"Oh no! That's terrible. Is he going to be okay?"

Marley walked down the sidewalk and continued her conversation, "Yeah, I think so. He's having surgery and it looks like his recovery time will be at least a few weeks. Probably longer."

"How awful!"

"I know. It is awful, but the bigger problem is he won't be able to cover his surgical practice, so…"

"So, your mom called you to see if you would do it?"

Marley waited for the crosswalk light to change and then crossed the street. "Bingo."

Tara chomped on her gum for a few seconds before speaking again, "So, what about partnership? Have you talked to your practice about leaving?"

Marley stepped out of the way of a fellow passerby and stopped walking once across the street. "I talked to Dr. Fortwright today, and he understood. He did tell me to check in with them and be available for phone calls and virtual consults if needed. I told him I hoped to return as soon as possible. If dad's recovery takes longer than six weeks or so, it might create a problem. I don't know. I can't think about that. I'm already dreading the return to the Hometown of Horrors. I can't let my mind add the threat of losing my partnership or job to the list of concerns. At least not right now."

"So, when do you leave?"

Shifting her weight, Marley stared at the ground. She focused on the crack in the sidewalk. "Saturday morning. Bright and early."

"Wow, that's soon. Well, we have to get together before you leave and have a send-off meal. What's your schedule like?"

Marley moved her phone to the other ear, her neck going into a crick. "I have to stop by the hospital in the morning for an hour or so. I need to check out my patients to Dr. Sloan, but after that, I'm free. Want to meet me for lunch and help me get supplies together? We could eat, shop, and head back to my townhouse to talk while I pack."

Tara didn't hesitate. "I'm there. Where should we meet for lunch?"

Marley scrunched her nose, thinking. "How about The Garden Table? It might be my last chance to eat good vegan food until I return. According to my mom, she's already baked her way into next week. She thinks vegan food means there is a vegetable present. And there's no convincing her otherwise. So, I may starve."

"Okay, The Garden Table it is. Though, I don't know why you adhere to this vegan diet. As my grandmother would say, 'You're as thin as a rail.'"

"I told you, it's not only about staying slim and fit. It's about overall health. You should try it. All that glitter and gum can't be good for you. Don't even get me started on your sugar- infused caramel, foam-topped, latte, mocha, whatever concoctions you order at The Bean. It should be a crime to consume so much sugar in one sitting."

Tara snorted. "Are you done? Ready to hop off that soapbox of yours?"

"I nag because I care."

"I know you do, and I love you for it. But I'm not giving up my delicious coffee drinks. Or the gum. So, back off."

Marley knew when she'd lost the battle. "Fine, fine. So, tomorrow at noon? If you get there first, go ahead and grab us a table."

"You got it. Oh, and Marley…"

Marley tilted her head. "Yeah, Tara?"

"Have fun checking out to Dr. Sloan tomorrow. Maybe you can pick up where you left off after your dinner." She proceeded to make kissing sounds into the phone.

"Not. Funny. Listen, one of these days, there's going to be a chance for payback, and—"

"Kidding! I'm kidding. Sort of—bye."

Before Marley had a chance to interject, her friend had ended the call. Marley lifted her head to the clear, blue sky above and whispered a silent prayer. She hoped her discussion with Dr. Sloan tomorrow would go smoothly. *Right.*

Chapter 5

December 13, 2019, Friday

Marley had overslept after a fitful night's sleep filled with dreams about walking into her high school on the first day of school wearing pajamas and unkempt hair. The scar on her forehead had grown in length and brightened in color.

As she walked down the hallway carrying her teddy bear named Oscar from her toddler days, the teenagers lining the halls whispered and pointed. At the end of the hallway stood Stacey and Charlie. They both wore matching sneers, and Stacey stepped forward. She teased, "Scarly Marley has a bear. Scarly Marley has frizzy hair." After the third round of this rousing chant, Marley's alarm blessedly blared, ending the horrifying dream sequence.

She jolted upright in her bed. Sweat beaded on the back of her neck, and nausea swept over her. *Ugh. Blackstone Haven. Stacey. Charlie.* Her mom's constant baking and unknowing criticism. Her father's stern expression and penchant for precision. *No mistakes.*

Marley placed both hands on her face and bowed her head. *God, how can I survive this? How can I face these people? That place? After all this time. I still feel like Scarly Marley. They won't think I'm anything else. I wasn't good enough then. How can I be good enough now?*

Glancing at her clock's red numbers, Marley realized she didn't have time to ponder the situation further. She sent a final, "Help me," to God and tossed her white down comforter off her body. She bolted out of bed and patted across the cool wood floor to the small bathroom attached to her bedroom.

She jumped in the shower, and the welcome rush of hot water pelted her face and neck, distracting her from the disturbing memories of her sleep. After standing under the spray and steam until the water turned cool, Marley hopped out and dressed in blue scrubs. She blew out her hair, creating smooth crimson waves, and pulled it back into a low ponytail. After smoothing her bangs over her scar and pinning them in place, she tossed on some makeup and felt ready for the day. Or at least as prepared as possible.

She dashed out her door, grabbing her black bag, charcoal wool coat and gloves, and phone on the way. After brushing off a fresh film of powdery snow from her windshield and driving through the traffic on the Beltway, Marley made it into the hospital only minutes before her scheduled time to round with Dr. Sloan.

As she scurried down the hallway toward the main surgical floor, she set her shoulders straight. *Professional. Remain professional.* She could do it. Staring at her shoes as she took each step, she didn't dodge the obstacle in her path.

Colliding with a body, Marley exclaimed, "Ouch."

"Not watching where you're going, are you Dr. Bakersfield? Or maybe you're looking for an excuse to land in my arms?" Dr. Sloan, his gelled hair and winning smile, raised a brow. He wore a white button-up shirt, a black tie, and a pair of unwrinkled charcoal dress pants.

Marley's face filled with blood, and words escaped her for a moment. When she gathered herself, she managed to utter an, "Uh." *Nice.* How clever of her.

"Uh to you, too. Are you ready to round so we can kick off the weekend? Maybe grab an early lunch together? It couldn't hurt to discuss the practice a little more, among other things."

Marley decided to play dumb. "Oh, yes. I mean, no. Yes, to the rounding, but no to the lunch. I'm sorry. I already have plans to meet a friend. You know her, actually, Dr. Madding? In pediatrics?" Why was she stating all of her sentences like a question? She tapped her foot, anxious to get this part of the day behind her. Not that Dr. Sloan wasn't handsome. He was. But something about him made her uneasy. She didn't know if it was his overconfidence, or his reputation with women, or that fact that seeing him on a personal level would complicate their working relationship. Maybe it was all of the above. Marley didn't want to get roped into another meal or date of any kind with him. Still, she didn't want to upset him, either. After all, he had a vote in determining her partnership in the practice.

"Oh, really? Well, that's a shame. Maybe another time. Perhaps, this weekend." He raised his brow higher.

How high would it go? "That is a nice invitation." *It was not.* "Unfortunately, the reason I'm checking out to you today is that I have to head home and help my parents for a few weeks."

He crossed his arms in front of his chest, and his eyes darkened. "Oh? I hadn't heard."

"I spoke with Dr. Fortwright yesterday. My dad had an unexpected accident, and he needs help at his practice. Plus, with Christmas coming, it seemed like a reasonable time to take some leave."

He frowned. "Well, I suppose that's true. Where is your hometown?"

"It's a few hours from here. A little place called Blackstone Haven. Lots of farms, horses, quaint shops. Bed and breakfasts. A few stoplights. That's about it."

Dr. Sloan shuddered. "Sounds horrible. At least you won't be gone long. Especially with partnership looming, right?"

Marley nodded. "Right."

Smoothing his tie with his hand, Dr. Sloan sent her a broad smile. "Great. I suppose we should get started, then. Any other surprises for the day?"

Marley's shoulders relaxed, and she gave him a small grin. "No, I think that's enough for one day. And the good news is the patient list doesn't look too full for the weekend. Should be a light call for you, Dr. Sloan."

He inched closer to her, closing the space between them. Lowering his voice, he spoke softly, "Jesse. I've told you before to call me Jesse." He extended a hand, waiting for her to give him a copy of the patient list.

She passed it to him and hesitated before responding, "Uh, I don't know if I could do that. At least, not until we are both partners."

He stepped closer, locking his eyes with hers. "I insist."

Marley's mouth went dry. "Well, if you insist. Okay, then." She broke away from his gaze, trying to put a few steps between them. "Jesse, why don't we start our rounds?"

He beamed and glanced at the patient list. "Sounds good. You lead the way."

Marley filled in Dr. Sloan-just-call-me-Jesse on the patients she'd been caring for and their treatment plans. Two hours later, she'd reviewed everything requiring attention in her absence. Standing in front of the nursing station on the hospital's third floor, Marley's stomach growled. She glanced at the clock on the wall and realized she needed to hurry if she didn't want to be late meeting Tara. She finished typing her final note on the computer and raised her eyes to meet Jesse's. "I hate to leave all this work for you and the practice to handle, but I appreciate your understanding."

He waved her away. "No problem. You're sure I can't convince you to have lunch with me instead?"

She shook her head. "I can't. In fact, if I don't leave right now, I'm going to leave Tara waiting. Thank you again. I promise to be back as soon as possible."

Jesse stared into her eyes and lowered his voice, "Sooner."

"Uh, right. Sure. Sooner." She had to get out of here, or he'd wriggle a dinner date out of her before she left town. Marley still didn't think seeing Jesse outside of the hospital promised anything other than complications and trouble. She logged off her account on the computer and rose from her seat. Keeping her eyes focused on gathering her pens and bag, she tossed him a quick, "Bye," and dashed toward the locker room to change.

Marley tossed on a fresh pair of black leggings and a long sleeve red top she'd stuffed in her bag earlier. She redid her ponytail and smoothed over her bangs. A quick inspection in the mirror left her satisfied the scar couldn't be seen. Fifteen minutes later, Marley strolled into The Garden Table.

The scent of fresh greens intermixed with mint tea tickled Marley's nose. She pulled in a breath. *Aah.* Her eyes fell upon Tara, waiting for her at a white lacquer table on the far side of the room. A light-up sign boasting the restaurant's name hung above the counter where patrons formed a queue to order. Lifting her hand, Marley waved at her best friend. She hurried to join her, and the two took their place in line.

Tara wore neon pink leggings and a white long sleeve fitted shirt underneath a puffy white down vest. She had her hair pulled high atop her head in a bun, and an ear warming band encircled her forehead. She flashed Tara a joyful smile and gave her a hug.

"So, how was your date, I mean, rounding with Dr. Sloan." A teasing glint twinkled in Tara's eyes before she turned to take a step forward in line.

Marley rolled her eyes. Talking to the back of Tara's head, she defended herself, "Ha-ha. You're hilarious, you know. And subtle. Really subtle. For your information, rounding went fine. Nothing unexpected…well…he did try to get me to go to lunch with him, but thankfully, I had plans with you, which I told him."

Tara spun around and raised her pointer finger in the air. "Aha. I knew it. He likes you. Dr. Sloan likes you; Dr. Sloan likes you," she sang in a sing-song fashion while hopping from one foot to the other like a kid playing hopscotch.

"What is wrong with you? Are you ten? He does not like me. We're not even going to entertain that as a possibility because, as you know, my life has imploded. Or exploded, whichever is worse, and I cannot, I repeat, cannot handle anything else right now. I have to go home, help my dad, try to keep the peace with both my parents, avoid eating all the non-vegan sugary concoctions my mother will bake, and dodge all the people from my past. Then, I need to return here as soon as possible to resume my perfect, beautiful life. In a beautiful city. With shiny, beautiful career goals. Nice and neat. So that's that."

Tara had reached the front of the line, but before she placed her order, she glanced over her shoulder at Marley. "You're sure?"

Marley narrowed her eyes and spoke in a warning tone, "I'm sure."

Instead of saying anything further on the matter, Tara whipped her head forward. She gave the guy behind the counter wearing a green apron her order. He punched the items into his tablet and shouted to a co-worker. "She wants double chocolate on the shake."

Marley shook her head. She and Tara couldn't be more different, but their friendship worked. No matter what happened in life, Tara always rushed to Marley's side to help as a loyal, if not over-sugared, friend.

The barista stared at Marley, waiting for her to order. "Uh, let's see. Please give me a smoothie with leafy greens, strawberries, banana, a side salad, and a grilled portabella burger with Dijon glaze. I want tomato, onion, artichoke, and olive tapenade on it. No bun."

His chin sagged as if he might not make it through the rest of his day, let alone her order.

She handed the man her credit card and waited while he processed it.

Tara leaned over and muttered out of the side of her mouth, "You know, if you don't order a bun, it's not technically called a burger."

Marley lightly shoved her friend down the line and grabbed her card back from the despondent barista.

The two women took a seat at an empty table, placed the number card on top of the table, and waited for their food. They chatted about Marley's upcoming adventure and what she needed to purchase. A few minutes later, a more perky blond worker arrived to deliver their food.

Marley nodded her thanks to the girl.

Tara lifted her chocolate-enriched shake in the air. "I propose a toast prayer."

Picking up her bright green cup of nutrients, Marley tilted her head. "What's a toast prayer?"

"It's where you make a big speech but turn it into a prayer." She smiled.

Marley grinned. "Okay, then, what are we toast-praying about?"

"To friendship, to new experiences, to your dad's healing, to your impending partnership, and to second chances. I'm praying God will open the door for you and your parents to have a positive visit and for you to see yourself the way He does—a beautiful, good-hearted woman. No matter what the people at Blackstone Haven might say.

Marley raised her head, and tears filled her eyes. She blinked them back. "Thanks, Tara. Cheers." She tapped her plastic cup against Tara's and grinned.

Marley took a long draw off her smoothie and dug into her non-burger burger. By the end of lunch, she'd filled her stomach, laughed until she cried, and made a list of all the things she needed to buy and pack this afternoon.

Tara tossed their trash away and rose from the table. "Ready to shop?"

Grinning, Marley stood and grabbed her bag off the back of her chair. "Do you even have to ask?"

Tara smiled and shook her head.

Following her friend out the cafe's front door, Marley prepared to her face her past.

~

Tara placed the umpteenth bag of bold roast coffee from The Bean into an open suitcase on Marley's bed. "I don't see how you're going to need this much coffee. And don't they have some sort of coffee shop in Blackstone Haven? They must."

Folding another pair of black pants, Marley tucked them into a suitcase. She tried to keep them from rubbing against her tennis shoes, a canister of flaxseed, and a jar of b12 vitamins.

Tara's gaze drifted from the suitcase she had been working on to Marley's health supplies. "I don't know how you take all that stuff every day." She stuck out her tongue and made a gagging sound.

"It's good for you. You should try it. You might discover you like something healthy. Besides, as a pediatrician, aren't you supposed to be setting a good example for your patients?" She stared at Tara.

Tara lifted both hands. "All right, all right. I surrender. Well, mostly. I'm not trying your health food concoctions, but I'll get off your case about it. Now, do you have everything you need?"

Marley referred to her list she'd made at lunch. "Let's see. I've got work clothes, scrubs, workout wear, dress shoes, tennis shoes…my health food as you call it, toiletries, makeup, and most importantly, coffee. Lots of coffee." She lifted her head and found her friend's eyes. "I think I'm ready. Or at least as ready as possible. I'm dreading the idea of bumping into someone from high school. Maybe between seeing patients and dodging my mother's guilt trips and my father's stern looks, I'll have no time left to run around town." She shrugged.

"That's the spirit. Way to see the glass half full. Loving the positivity." Her mouth settled into a straight line. "Seriously, though, I'll be praying for you, and if anyone gives you any trouble, I'm only a phone call away. Who knows? I might pop down to visit one weekend that I'm not on call. Try to enjoy the time with your family. I'm sure all those people from high school have grown up and matured."

Marley snorted. "Yeah, I'm sure."

Tara raised her fist in the air and shook it. "Positivity."

Marley matched her gesture, although with less enthusiasm. She felt positive about one thing—this entire venture could become a train wreck, and she'd return from her hometown feeling more like Scarly Marley than ever before. Marley sighed. Instead of speaking those words aloud to her optimistic friend, she pasted a forced smile on her face. "Positivity."

Chapter 6

December 14, 2019, Saturday

Marley shoved her small black medical bag in the corner of one of her suitcases and zipped it shut. *There, that should do it.* She felt confident she'd packed everything in her townhouse inside the luggage. The bags groaned at the pressure against the zippers, but they held.

Ringing from her cell phone broke her consternation over her suitcases' ability to remain shut during the trip. She bent down and dug the phone out of her purse, before standing as she answered, "Hi Mom."

"Marley, I wanted to see when you if you were on the road yet and what time you'd arrive."

Marley glanced at the alarm clock on her nightstand. *12:15 p.m.* "I'm about to load the rest of my things in the car, and then I'm all set. As long as traffic isn't a nightmare on the I-270, I should make it there by 2:00 p.m. at the latest. Maybe 2:30."

She could hear her mom's footsteps pacing in the background. "Okay, well, your dad's surgery got bumped to this morning. There was another emergency last night. They just took him back. The doctor said it would be at least a few hours, and he would send someone to update me periodically."

Picking up her purse, Marley slung it over her shoulder, keeping her phone wedged between her neck and the other shoulder. "I'll drive to the hospital, then."

"Oh, you don't have to do that, Honeybun."

Honeybun. It had been her mother's pet name for her since Marley could remember. Her mom said it in love, but it reminded Marley of the other kids teasing her about her weight. The middle schooler's snide comments about how Marley earned the nickname because of her resultant plump figure from the honeybuns she consumed at lunch still stung upon hearing the name. *Kids can be cruel.*

"It's not a problem, Mom. I'll drive straight there, and that way, I can check on Dad after surgery. I'd feel better if I got to speak to his physician myself, anyway. And it will give me a chance to check in with the human resource department and make sure everything is ready for me to start seeing patients Monday."

"Alright. That's great. I'd appreciate the company. Be safe on the road, and make sure you get something to eat. I made you a cake and put a roast in the crockpot, but we might not return to the house until late, and I hate to think of you starving to death. The last time I laid eyes on you, I thought the wind might blow you away."

"Mom, that's thoughtful of you, but like I told you the other day, I don't eat meat and—"

"Oh, Honeybun, I've got to go. I see one of the surgical nurses coming this way. I want to make sure they don't need me for something. See you soon. Bye."

Her mother hung up and ended the discussion about the dinner menu. Shaking her head, Marley scurried to her kitchen. Opening the white cabinet above the stove, she pulled out a box of vegan granola bars. Staring at the box for a moment, she debated. *Better grab two.* She yanked out an extra box and ran back to her bedroom.

She shoved the sustenance into her purse and slung it back over her shoulder again, grabbing the larger suitcase from her bed. Heaving it to the floor, Marley then lifted the second one off as well. Clasping their handles, she spun around and dragged them behind her.

As she stood at the door to her townhouse, ready to leave, she paused and looked around her living room. A sigh escaped, and then she straightened her posture and nodded. She could do this.

Opening the door, Marley pulled her suitcases through and shut it behind her. She lugged them out to her car and loaded them in the trunk. As she slipped inside the driver's seat of her car, Marley bowed her head and whispered a prayer, "God, help me." Searching for the rest of the words within her heart, she couldn't muster anything else. "Please, help me." And with her final plea, she backed out of her driveway and drove away from her current life, ready to face the past.

~

Weaving in and out of traffic on the I-270 N from Washington, D.C. toward Blackstone Haven left Marley's hands tired from gripping the steering wheel. Her eyes hung heavy from the fierce concentration on the horrible driving antics of her fellow commuters.

As she pulled into Blackstone Haven, Marley had one thought—coffee. She needed it. And lots of it. Her stomach growled—and maybe one of her vegan granola bars, too.

Driving down the main street on the way to the hospital, she saw the big oval sign hanging above a brick building heralding The Baking Grind: Coffee and Sweets. Marley slowed her car to a near-stop. She remembered that place--it had been around since she was in elementary school. The lady that owned it always wore pearls and a white apron over a knee-length dress. She'd had a kind smile and a free cookie for any kid that entered her establishment.

Marley pulled her car into an empty spot lining the street and put it in park. Grabbing her purse, she stepped outside and slammed the door behind her. She shuffled in her bag for loose change and fed the black meter. No reason to start this adventure with a parking ticket as a homecoming gift.

She smoothed out her white dress shirt and dark skinny jeans and patted her hair to ensure no loose tendrils had escaped her ponytail. Looking both ways before crossing the street,

Marley took hurried steps to avoid getting struck. *Not that there was any traffic in Blackstone Haven.*

Placing her hand on the store's door handle, she yanked the door open and met the reward of a butter, sugar, and dark roast perfume. She could do without the sweets, but the promise of caffeine encouraged her.

The bakery case held countless cakes, cookies, bagels, and pies--all visible through the clear glass. Behind the counter remained empty, with no waitstaff in view. Marley took a few steps forward, and her charcoal high-heeled boots resonated on the floor. "Hello? Is anyone here?"

With no response, Marley inched forward. A small white placard with gold engravement sat next to a golden bell and said, "Ring for Service." She raised her hand above the bell and looked around the empty space again. She hated to bother anyone, but the need for coffee had reached a desperate level, so she tapped the top of the bell with her palm—*ding ding.*

From a backroom emerged the most handsome man Marley had seen. Ever. He had dark wavy hair that hung slightly over his eyes. He ran his hand through it, pushing it out of the way in a smooth manner that caused her knees to weaken. His eyes shone a royal blue, and when he raised them to meet hers, his lips broke into a wide smile that quickened her pulse.

"Hi Marley, it's great to see you again. I heard about your dad, and I wondered if you might come to town for a while." He wiped his hands on a towel while he spoke, then extended a hand toward her.

Marley narrowed her eyes. "How do you know my name?"

The gorgeous stranger stood with his hand still outstretched and grinned wider. His eyes twinkled. "I'd recognize you anywhere. Doesn't matter if it's been almost twenty years; that red hair and those emerald eyes are unmistakable. You're still as beautiful as you were back in third grade."

Marley's tongue had stuck to the roof of her mouth, and she found she couldn't speak. *Benjamin...from grade school. Wow, he'd grown up.* "Benjamin? Benjamin Miller? Is that you?"

"It's me. How's your dad?" He shoved up the rolled-up sleeves of his grey shirt and stepped closer to the counter, resting his hands on the glass display.

Marley became acutely aware of his firm, muscular forearms before her, and warmth traveled from her chest upward, settling in her cheeks. Pulling her eyes away from this distraction, she met his gaze and chastised herself. *Act professionally, respectfully. Stop this nonsense.* It was no use. Her cheeks continued to burn. "Uh, my dad? Oh, I don't know, actually. I mean, that sounds terrible. That's not what I meant. I'm on my way to the hospital to check on him, but I stopped here for a quick coffee. After driving in from D.C., I needed a pick-me-up."

He sent her another warm smile. "Well, let's get you that pick-me-up. What can I get you?"

Marley shifted her eyes toward the display case below and inspected its offerings. The rows of pastry placed upon white paper doilies and brightly colored plates called to her, but she refused to give in to the sugary temptation. After a few seconds, she lifted her head and cleared her throat. Thankfully, her tongue cooperated. "I'll have a black coffee." She reached into her purse and pulled out her wallet.

Benjamin lifted one hand. "Please, put that away. It's on the house. But are you sure all you want is a black coffee? No cream and sugar? No latte? What about one of my mother's famous cinnamon rolls?"

"No, the coffee is fine." Marley placed her wallet back inside her purse and shook her head. "How is your mom? She was always so sweet to me."

The smile vanished from Benjamin's face. "Oh, your mom didn't tell you?"

Marley's heart fell into her stomach. "Tell me what?"

"My mom passed away a few years ago. Right after I finished culinary school. I had a job lined up at Premier in New York City, but Mom had a heart attack and needed me to come home and take care of her and the bakery, so..." Benjamin shrugged.

Marley whispered, "Duty calls." She nodded. "I get it. Same for me. I have a great partnership waiting for me in D.C., but my mom called to tell me about Dad's fall, and here I am." She dropped her head for a few seconds before raising it to find Benjamin's eyes again. "I'm sorry about your mom, Benjamin."

"She made it a few months after the first heart attack. Did rehab, worked hard on getting better. She even gave up sugar, which was a big deal for her. I thought we'd made it over the major hurdles, but I came to the bakery to open one morning, and when I went home for lunch to check on her..." Benjamin's eyes glistened with tears. He turned away from her, busying himself with filling her coffee cup from the massive black machine behind him.

"Benjamin, I'm so sorry."

He snapped a black lid on top of the green paper coffee in silence before turning around. Finding Marley's eyes again, he sent her a half-smile. "It's okay. Not your fault. And it's been several years. I'm doing well. After she passed, I stayed here to run the bakery, and I always intended to sell it and return to big city life as a pastry chef, but...what can I say, this town is home." He handed over her coffee.

She picked up the cup and gave a slow nod. "Right. Home." *If home could be called a place of past torture and pain, then sure.*

Her face must have betrayed her words because Benjamin lifted one brow. "You okay?"

"Yeah, I need to get to the hospital. I have a lot to do if I'm going to see patients on Monday, and I want to make sure my Dad is doing well, too."

Benjamin nodded. "I'll keep your Dad in my prayers. And if you change your mind about those cinnamon rolls, you know where to find me."

Marley's heart pounded. "Right. I know where to find you." She let her eyes linger for a few seconds longer before turning to leave. As she approached the door with her head lowered, it opened before she could reach for the handle.

A thick, syrupy voice caused Marley's head to snap up. "I cannot believe what my eyes are seeing. Is that little Scarly Marley? Well, now you're little. I guess we all know back in the day that wasn't true." The speaker patted Marley on the arm. "I'm only kidding, honey. Or was it Honeybun? Isn't that what your mother called you?"

The words hit Marley like a bucket of ice water, and her blood ran cold. "Stacey. Stacey Blackstone." She couldn't bring herself to utter the words, "It's good to see you," because frankly, it wasn't. Marley remained honest if nothing else.

"In the flesh." She tossed her shiny, blond head back and laughed.

Marley forced herself to hide a shudder. Somehow in a matter of seconds, Stacey had made her feel two inches tall. "I see. Well, if you don't mind, I need to run..."

"Oh, off to the hospital, I imagine."

Marley's jaw dropped. News sure traveled fast around here. Blackstone Haven's gossip mill could put any social media platform to shame when it came to information and gossip distribution. "As a matter of fact, yes."

Stacey flashed her toothy homecoming queen grin.

For a moment, Marley thought she might add the wave and burst into an acceptance speech.

"My daddy told me you were coming to town. I thought he'd made it up. It seems like none of us have seen you since graduation night. You slip into town and slip out like a stealth ninja."

"I don't know if I'd put it that way. I've come home for holidays, but I—"

Stacey stepped closer, and her eyes widened. She placed a hand on her chest. "And when I heard what happened to your poor father…well, I assumed you'd come to the rescue. Of course, no one would blame him if he wanted to retire and sell his practice. He's certainly earned the right. My daddy says Blackstone Hospital offered your father a big sum to buy him out, but he turned them down." She dropped her head closer to Marley's face and lowered her voice. "Maybe you can convince him to reconsider. I'd imagine with his injury he's going to need lots of rest. And life is short. Isn't that what they say?"

Marley clenched her fists but kept her arms at her side. Stacey's father owned almost everything in Blackstone Haven, including the hospital. "I don't know who 'they' are, but if I know my father, he's tough and not likely to give up the patients he's cared for most of his life or the practice he's built from the ground up—that's why I'm here. To make sure things run smoothly. I stopped in for a coffee, but now I really must go. My mother will be expecting me. And as you said, I need to see how my father's doing, too."

Stacey looked Marley up and down. "Hmm. Well, let him know I'm sure the offer still stands. And send him my best." She raised an arm in the air and waved toward the counter. "Hello, Ben! Good morning. I see you're working hard." She cast Benjamin a smile before sharing a conspiratorial whisper with Marley, "I bet you were shocked to see how well little Bennie Miller grew up."

Marley's face flushed, and she forced herself to control her voice, "Oh, I hadn't noticed. I mean, I noticed he grew up, obviously, but I didn't talk to him long. Just ordered my coffee." She lifted her cup in the air as proof.

Stacey leaned in again, "Well, between you and me, I plan to make myself Mrs. Miller."

Raising her brow, Marley attempted to keep the look of shock and disappointment off her face. "Oh, really? How long have you two been dating?"

She whispered once more, "We're not. Yet. But I'm working on it." She stood up straight and held the door open for Marley. "I hope you have a blessed day, Scarly Marley—oh, I'm sorry, I meant, Marley. Tell your parents I said hello."

Squaring her shoulders back, Marley hiked her purse higher and lifted her chin. *Ignore her. She's only trying to get a response.* "Thank you, Stacey. Goodbye." And with those parting words, Marley walked out the door, leaving her childhood tormentor behind her. *For now.* She gulped in a breath of fresh air and released it. *It. Would. Be. Okay. She hoped. Maybe. Oh, who was she kidding? It might be a total disaster, but she was committed.*

Marley jogged to her car and hopped inside. Shoving the keys in the ignition, she started it and whipped into the non-existent traffic, heading to the hospital. Glancing at the clock, she saw she'd only been in the bakery for fifteen minutes. Fifteen minutes that felt like an eternity. She shook her head. *This day has to get better. Please, God, let it get better.* And with this final prayer, she sped to Blackstone Hospital to face her parents.

Chapter 7

December 14, 2019, Saturday

Benjamin watched Marley Bakersfield jet out of the bakery like her feet were on fire after her conversation with Stacey Blackstone. He'd overheard Stacey's parting words, "Scarly Marley." Shaking his head, he thought back to all the times in elementary and middle school when the neighborhood kids had teased Marley. He doubted they'd tease her now.

Even though her long, red locks appeared smoother and her figure leaner, he'd recognize those brilliant emerald eyes anywhere. They held kindness, goodness, and strength not found within many people he'd met.

He gave the counter one final swipe and then slung the towel over his shoulder. Raising his head, his eyes caught the gaze of Marley's tormenter approaching the counter. His heart plummeted, and he busied himself with straightening the white and black mugs to the right side of the counter, trying to avoid the conversation to come. Stacey had made no secret of her interest in him, though he had no intention of reciprocating her feelings. He heard the click-clack of her heels, and his heart rate increased. *And not in a good way.*

"Why Benjamin Miller, you've hardly spoken to me since I walked through the door. Is that any way to treat a loyal customer?"

Benjamin stopped fiddling with the mugs and darted his eyes toward Stacey. *Remain professional. Treat her like a paying customer. Take her order, and then maybe she'll leave.* It wasn't that Stacey Blackstone wasn't beautiful; quite the opposite. Her looks rivaled those of a model or a Hollywood star. She had long blond hair, blue eyes, and a fit physique from daily sessions at the gym...but that's where her attributes ended. While her exterior appeared pleasing, her heart was not. At least not to him. She'd teased and bullied others all her life to get what she wanted, a tactic he imagined she'd learned from her father. No, she couldn't be more different from someone like Marley.

Stacey tapped on the glass counter with her red-polished nails. They looked like daggers. *At least they matched her personality.* The thought made the corner of his mouth turn upward on one side.

She tapped again. "Well?"

He snapped to attention. "I'm sorry, Stacey, what did you say?"

Splashing on her fake grin, she batted her eyelashes at him. "I said, is that any way to treat little ol' me?"

Clearing his throat, he stood taller and went into bakery owner mode. "What can I get you, Stacey?"

She leaned down to inspect the pastries in the display below and scrutinized her choices. "Hmm, let's see...I think I'll have an apple turnover and a café latte...oh, and one of those blueberry scones. Blueberry scones are my daddy's favorite. I think I'll pop over to see him and momma... I'm sure he'll be interested to know Scarly Marley made it to town. Her poor father." She turned her mouth downward into a frown that didn't look sincere.

"Yes, it's a terrible thing, him getting hurt. Thankfully, he has Marley to help him out right now. By the way, I don't think you should call her Scarly Marley anymore. It's not the nicest nickname, Stacey."

Stacey placed a hand on his forearm and sent him a teasing grin. "Oh, you know I'm kidding. It's mostly out of habit. Hard to believe she's back in town. Of course, it won't last. A few weeks from now and I'm sure she'll be bored out of her mind and headed back to the big city. Besides, she knows I don't mean it."

He doubted Marley knew that. And he thought she probably did mean it, but he wasn't going to argue any further with Stacey. He wanted to give her the pastries she'd requested and get her out of his shop. Benjamin placed the turnover and scone in a white paper bag and stapled the top shut with force. Turning around, he started to pour her tea into a to-go cup. With his back still to Stacey, he asked, "Do you need anything else?"

"Well, since you asked…why don't you and I partner up for the upcoming Blackstone Haven Valentine's Day dance committee?"

He jumped, nearly burning his hand on the stream of hot water. Wincing, he sat Stacey's cup down and grabbed his hand, applying pressure. When the stinging subsided, he shoved the plastic lid on the cup and formulated a response in his head.

Turning to Stacey, Benjamin placed her tea and bag of pastries on the counter in front of her. "Wow, Stacey, thanks for the invite, but I don't know if I'll be attending the dance this year or not. Valentine's Day is a busy day here at the bakery, but I'm sure you can find someone else to help you."

"Well, if you change your mind…" She picked up her order and sent him a final flirtatious grin and eyelash bat.

Ugh. He would not be changing his mind. "Uh, thanks, but I really do have a lot of work around here."

"Okay, but I haven't given up on you, Benjamin Miller. Are you going to participate in the Chamber of Commerce's New Year's Eve Bakeoff?"

Benjamin had planned to attend the bake-off this year—it had been a town tradition. In fact, his mother held the record for most years won. Plus, it was for a good cause--the net proceeds benefited the children's floor at the hospital. "You know, I'm not sure. That's a busy time of year for the bakery business, too."

"If you do decide to join, let me know if you need a helper. The rules say you can enter with a partner this year. My father said an anonymous donor promised a sizable cash prize to the winner with a matching donation to the children's floor. Think of what your bakery could become with a little cash infusion." And with this final piece of news, she sashayed toward the door.

An idea formed in Benjamin's mind. He considered what his bakery might become with some equity. *It could be great.* As wonderful as any of the French patisseries he'd trained in during culinary school. Not to mention, he struggled to keep the doors open most months. Since the passing of his mother, he'd tried to keep the business in the black. His mother had a giving spirit and generous heart--so generous she gave away more items than she got paid for most weeks.

Lost in his thoughts, he didn't realize Stacey hadn't left yet until she trilled, "Think about it. Bye, Benjamin," and sauntered out the door.

He hated to admit that Stacey Blackstone might be right about something, but she was this time. He would definitely think about it.

Chapter 8

December 14, 2019, Saturday

Marley pulled into the hospital parking lot and slammed on her emergency brake. She pulled the keys out of the ignition and tossed them in her purse, sliding out the driver's side. She closed the door and waited for the automatic locking mechanism to make its characteristic beep.

Jogging to the hospital's front door, she said a silent prayer. *God, please let my dad be okay, and please give me the words to say to my mom.* The small community hospital in her hometown only had three floors. She stepped on the elevator and rode it up to the third floor. As she exited the elevator, she nearly plowed over her mom. "Oh, sorry, Mom. I didn't see you there. How's Dad?"

"Honeybun! Give me a hug." She embraced her daughter in a tight squeeze before releasing her. "I haven't seen you in ages. You look too thin." She pinched and prodded at Marley's arms, inspecting them. "Are you eating? As soon as we get home, I'm going to feed you something."

Marley smoothed out her shirt again. "I'm not skin and bones, Mom. I eat, I promise. But you didn't answer my question. How is Dad doing?"

Marley's mother grabbed her by the hand. "Why don't you come to see for yourself. He got out of surgery and did well. He's a little groggy still, but that's to be expected, I suppose."

Following her mom down the small hallway to her father's hospital room, Marley couldn't help but notice the difference between this hospital and her facility in D.C. The hospital was nice--it smelled of fresh bleach, and there wasn't a speck of dirt or dust in sight, but everything looked smaller. Smaller hallway, smaller rooms, smaller beds. Still, everyone she'd passed smiled, nodded, and held doors for her.

Walking into her Dad's room, she noted how weak her father looked lying in bed. As a colonel in the army and standing at 6'2", his stature usually commanded a room and demanded instant respect. Now, covered in the white hospital sheet and blankets, he looked like a frail shell of his former self.

His tanned faced appeared more lined than the last time she'd seen him, and his buzz cut had grown out slightly with a wash of silver at his temples. He lay with his eyes closed, his chest rising evenly with each breath.

Marley found herself staring at his body, mesmerized by his respiration. Her throat tightened as she thought about how many years had crept upon her father's age. *He wouldn't be around forever.* She should make more of an effort to come home and visit--even if it was hard at times. Even with all the past pain.

She stood in silence with her mother for a few seconds. Marley turned to slip out the door when her mother stepped closer to the bed, placing a hand on her father's arm.

"Walter, honey. Walter, wake up. Someone is here to see you."

Marley's father opened his eyes and looked at her mother. He sent her a stiff smile and scanned the room. When his gaze fell upon Marley, his face lit up. His smile softened, and he cleared his throat. "Marley. Good of you to come. Glad to see you."

Marley debated whether to rush to her father's bedside and give him a giant hug or hang back. He'd never been big on public displays of emotion, and her childhood often ran with the structure and order of an army unit.

"Well, don't stand there. Come here. Let me inspect you." He waved her over with a slight lift of the hand closest to Marley.

She inched forward with slow, unsure steps. Reaching a hand toward her father's Marley kept her eyes focused on it.

He took it in his and gave it a squeeze. "You look good, Kid."

She squeezed back and lifted her eyes to meet his. "Thanks, Dad. How are you feeling?"

"Oh, you know me. Nothing can keep me down for long. My doctor told me I might be out of commission for up to 12 weeks, but I told him he doesn't know who he's dealing with here. I'm tough, and I'll be back up and working in six, eight weeks tops. If I survived a nine-month deployment overseas, then I'm sure I can endure a few weeks of orthopedic recovery."

"Dad, when I talked to Mom, she said she thought you'd need me for a few weeks, maybe six at the most. I don't want to rush your recovery, and I do want to help you, but—"

"Good, good. Good to hear. You know what I always say—"

"I know, I know. Duty calls."

"That's right, young lady. God, honor, duty, and family. That's what matters." He gave a firm nod of his head.

"And it does, Dad, but I told my work that I'd—"

Her father interrupted again, "Plastic surgery. Plastic surgery." He shook his head. "Now, general surgery, that's where you belong. With me, working in your hometown. Giving back to your community. Helping your fellow man. Not improving the faces of D.C.'s high society." His mouth turned down in obvious displeasure.

"Dad." Marley paused, trying to keep her composure. "I take care of burn victims, conduct facial reconstructions, repair cleft palates, and build self-esteem. The work I do is important. A lot of it provides a functional necessity for the patient." Marley's career was one area of her life that gave her confidence. She knew she performed well as a surgeon and that what she did changed lives.

He waved away her argument. "Yes, yes. You're saving the world. Meanwhile, I'm trying to save Blackstone Haven. Have you heard about the big hospital conglomerate? Somehow a huge corporation got tied up with Mr. Blackstone and now the hospital has set its eyes on my practice."

Marley's mother patted her father again. "Now, Walter. Don't start on that right now. You need your rest, and you're going to work yourself into a fit."

Leaning up on one elbow, Marley's father lifted his head from the pillow. "Sally, it's not right what those people are trying to do. To steal away the practice—my practice. From me. It's not right, and I won't stand for it. Not to mention how they don't know what's best

48

for my patients. I'm the one who has been caring for this community for years. And another thing—"

Marley's mother met Marley's eyes. She sent Marley a worried frown. "It's the same thing every time you bring it up. He'll go on a verbal bender for the better part of the next hour."

Marley sent her mother a small nod. "Dad. You're absolutely right, I'm sure. Why don't we shelve this topic until tomorrow? I promise you can tell me all about the Big Bad Company and Mr. Blackstone then. I need to get Mom home, and you need to rest. Especially if you're going to hold a scalpel in eight weeks or less."

Acceptance filled her father's eyes, and his jaw went slack. He relaxed his head on the pillow and closed his eyes. "I suppose you're right. And I will be ready by then. Or sooner. Take your mother home. Let her get some food in you. You're wasting away."

Marley rolled her eyes. The extra five pounds she chronically carried in her hips as part of her genetic inheritance begged to differ with his argument, but she let her father's comment slide. "Get some rest, Dad."

He made an almost imperceptible affirmation with his head, and Marley and her mother slipped out the hospital room door.

Marley turned to her mother once in the hallway. "He looks good. Seems as sharp as usual. I don't know how realistic it is for him to expect to be back to work in such a short timeframe, though. What will he do when I have to leave?"

Marley's mother patted her shoulder. "Now, Honeybun, let's not talk about that right now. For the time being, you are here. And I'm so happy to have my girl home." She lifted a strand of Marley's hair in her hand and inspected the ends. "Although, Honeybun, I do hate to criticize…"

"Then don't, Mom."

"But," sending Marley a pointed look, she continued, "your hair could use a trim. When was the last time you visited the salon? Are you taking care of yourself in that big city, or do you work all the time?"

Pulling her hair away from her mom, Marley forced her voice to remain even, "I'm fine, Mom. Really. I've been busier than usual recently with the partnership stuff on the table. I'm trying to prove myself, and this is a crucial time. And my hair does not need a trim."

That wasn't entirely true. It probably could use a snip. "And I'm not too thin."

"Well, we can agree to disagree. But enough of that for now. Let's head home. I've got all kinds of goodies made for you, and I cannot wait to sit down. My legs are aching."

Marley shook her head. Sometimes talking to her mom felt like talking to the wall. She knew her mother loved her, but Marley had no doubt that when she walked through the door to her childhood home, her nostrils would be assaulted with a sugary butter combo of all things non-vegan. "Okay, Mom, let's go." Marley followed her mother out of the hospital and into the parking lot toward another visit with her past.

~

Marley spent Sunday unpacking her things in her childhood bedroom. She'd tucked away shirts, pants, and undergarments into the battered dresser. After lining up her sneakers and heels inside her small closet, she placed her makeup and toiletries on an empty shelf in her bathroom.

The house in which she grew up looked unchanged since Marley had left for college. The three-bedroom, two-and-a-half-bathroom ranch-style home appeared modest considering her father's occupation and salary. But that was her father—practical, frugal, prudent. And anything else stoic and responsible. He didn't find the need to splurge where it wasn't necessary. In fact, she suspected if her father's seventeen-year-old sedan hadn't stopped going in reverse, he never would have purchased a new vehicle. *Yep, that's right—it would not go in reverse.* His favorite motto was, "A penny saved is a penny earned."

After dodging her mother's attempts to shove roast beef, muffins, and various other unhealthy things in her mouth, Marley claimed fatigue, took a shower and tucked herself into bed by 8:00 p.m. As she lay still, staring at the popcorn ceiling overhead, Marley thought about her best friend. She needed a dose of encouragement. Grabbing her phone off the nightstand, Marley punched in Tara's number and listened to the ringing.

Her best friend's upbeat voice echoed through the line, "Hey, girl. How's it going in the good ol' hometown?"

"Oh, peachy. So far, I've had a blast-from-the-past run-in with Stacey Blackstone and checked on my father. He's doing well considering...oh, and I'm trying to avoid the artery-clogging fare my mother insists on offering me every ten minutes. And now, I'm planted in the same bed I slept in every night, awaiting the torture Blackstone Haven High School promised me each day. So, that's how it's going. What about you?"

"Oh, forget about me. So, Stacey Blackstone...is she the girl that gave you a hard time in school?"

"The one and the same. Shiny blond hair, blue eyes, perfect figure. All still the same. A wicked twinkle in her eyes as she plots your demise. Yep, check. She reminded me of my childhood nickname, calling me Scarly Marley in front of Benjamin. Then she pointed out all the challenges that await me with my father's practice."

"Wait a minute, hold up. You totally glossed over the most interesting information. Benjamin? Who's Benjamin?"

Marley's face warmed as she pictured his deep blue eyes and dazzling smile. She lost herself in her daydream about the handsome baker.

"Marley? Marley? Do you hear me?"

"Huh? Oh, sorry. What were you saying?"

"I asked who Benjamin was, and then you went into some kind of trance, so I'm guessing he's hot."

"Really, Tara, do you have to be so blunt?"

"Ooh, no denial. That means he's super-hot." She cackled.

Marley picked at her pink and white comforter. "Well, he's not unfortunate looking. I'll say that. Benjamin owns a bakery in town. I stopped by there this morning to grab a coffee and spoke with him. He was the one kid from my neighborhood who treated me with any kindness. But from talking to Stacey, I think she has her eyes set on him. And I'm only here for a short time, so there's no point in going there, Tara."

"Oh, I don't know. I could see a point. For one thing, you might fall in love and find true happiness."

"I'm happy."

"Right. You sound ecstatic."

"I'm happy enough."

"Marley, you spend all your time working, and when you're not working, you're eating weeds and jogging five million miles a day. I hate to say it…but that doesn't sound too fun to me."

"We can't all get away with eating bubblegum and wearing glitter."

"Life is all about choices. Keep an open mind. Promise me you'll stop by the bakery every morning for your daily caffeine fix—which I know you'll need anyways."

Marley rolled her eyes. "You're hopeless, you know?"

"Oh and keep me updated. I want to hear all the details about the gorgeous baker. Maybe I'll swing down to visit you in the next few weeks and scope out this guy myself."

"Great. Exactly what I need—you coming to tease me in person. You'll have me married off in a matter of days."

"You know it."

Marley rolled onto her left side, facing away from the frosted window in her bedroom. Thinking about her conversation with Stacey again made her shiver. She pulled her comforter up over her shoulder. "Tara?"

"Yeah, Marley?"

"I miss you. I really do wish you were here. Something about being back here in this town, in this room, in this bed makes me feel like that chubby, frizzy-haired little girl with the scar on her forehead. I feel alone." Tears filled Marley's eyes, and this time she didn't hold them back. She sniffled.

Tara softened her voice, "Hey, don't cry. It's going to be okay--and you're not alone. You have God, and you have me. Seriously, if that girl gives you any more trouble, you call me, and I'll be there in a flash. And I was kidding about the guy. Well, sort of. I do think you should let down your guard and let some people in to know the real Marley because she's pretty great."

Marley sighed. "Thanks, Tara. You're the best. And do come down some weekend if you can get the days off. I'd love that."

"You got it, babe. I'll talk to you soon. Call me this week and let me know how the clinic goes. Did you get things finalized with the hospital about your credentialing?"

"Yeah, I'm ready." She hoped. "Tomorrow starts my first day as Blackstone Haven's newest surgical locum tenens."

"Hey, Blackstone Haven…the town isn't named after Stacey, is it?"

"Oh, that's another fun piece of news I guess I never shared with you before. Aside from being my childhood tormenter, Stacey is heir to the Blackstone fortune. Her family owns nearly everything major in this town. And if they don't own it, they hold stock in it, lease it, or put it out of business. Her father sits on the board of Blackstone Hospital, and he's the one pushing for my father to sell the practice."

"Why would he care one way or the other what happened to your dad's practice?"

"I don't know for sure, but my whole life, it seemed like Mr. Blackstone didn't like my father, and therefore Stacey never liked me. So, visiting my hometown…fun. Super fun."

Tara remained silent for a few seconds.

"Tara? Are you still there?"

"Yeah, I was praying for you."

Marley's shoulders relaxed and a sense of peace flowed over her. "Thanks."

"No problem. Listen, don't let those Blackstones make you feel bad or push you around. You are a wonderful, beautiful person, and God loves you. You don't have to sink to their level but stand up for yourself. Okay?"

Buoyed by her friend's encouragement, Marley nodded in the darkened room. "Okay."

"I'll talk to you later this week. Love you, girl."

"Love you, too. Bye." Marley set the alarm on her phone and placed it on the nightstand. She fluffed her pillow and settled her head on it once more. Closing her eyes, she tried to imagine her first day in the clinic going smoothly, but the memory of Stacey calling her Scarly Marley lingered. After thirty minutes of tossing from side to side, Marley sank into a fitful night's sleep.

Chapter 9

December 16, 2019, Monday

Marley pulled into the small parking lot in front of her father's medical practice. An old-fashioned wooden sign with hunter green lettering hung from the roof over the porch, and three wooden steps led to the historical home's front door.

She glanced out her car window at the sign's words, Dr. Bakersfield, and noted the irony that she'd be stepping into the role with the same name. Pulling in a deep breath, she held it for a few seconds before releasing it. She darted her eyes to the rearview mirror and angled it down with one hand so she could inspect her reflection.

Like always, her eyes immediately flew to the light scar on her forehead. She pressed her fingers to it and closed her eyes. *A few weeks.* She could do it. Opening her eyes, Marley smoothed her hair over the scar. Each morning, Marley applied a thick layer of cover-up to the mark, but even the best camouflage faded throughout the day. Once satisfied it had been covered, she grabbed her purse.

Marley exited the car and slammed the door. She righted herself and took the few steps up to the porch and front door. Her footsteps sounded more confident than she felt. Pulling out the key her mother had given her to the building, Marley slipped it into the deadbolt but found the door already unlocked. She turned the knob and pushed the door forward. Marley poked her head inside and looked around. "Hello? Is someone here?"

"Marley? Marley Bakersfield? Is that you?"

Marley's gaze flew to the source of the voice, and her eyes landed upon an elderly woman with a silver bob sitting behind a mahogany desk at the end of the hallway. She walked inside and closed the door behind her. "Excuse me? Who are you?"

"Why, Marley, has it been so long you don't even recognize your old Sunday school teacher?"

Marley squinted. The woman wore a cerulean and white floral blouse, a matching blue cardigan, and a string of pearls around her neck. She had thin, wire-rimmed glasses and a sweet smile. "Mrs. Klingensmith?"

"That's me. Didn't your father tell you?"

She sent her former Sunday school teacher a small smile. "Tell me what?"

"That I've been helping him around here? I'm his secretary. I started working in the office a few months ago. His last secretary left over a year ago, and he'd been trying to manage on his own. Occasionally, your mother stepped in to help, but with running the house and trying to cover here, it was a lot of work."

Marley walked forward and extended her hand. "I see. Well, it's good to see you again."

Mrs. Klingensmith rose from her seat and scooted around the desk. "Put that hand away and give me a hug. I'm going to be your right-hand woman for the coming weeks." She wrapped her arms around Marley and squeezed tight.

"Mrs. Klingensmith," Marley groaned.

The woman crushed her further. "What is it, Marley?"

"I can't breathe."

Mrs. Klingensmith released her from the embrace. "Oh, I'm sorry. Sometimes I get carried away and don't know my own strength. My granddaughter tells me the same thing. You'll meet her later. I told her to swing by after school. I think you'll like her. She reminds me of you."

"That's nice. I don't know if I'll be here or not, though. It depends on how the day goes and what's going on at the hospital. But I'm sure she's lovely."

"She is sweet. Well, I don't want to keep you. Busy day ahead. I looked at the patient list already and," the secretary whistled before continuing, "it's a doozy. I hope you got your caffeine fix this morning. You're going to need it."

Marley's stomach growled, and her head pounded. She hadn't had time to make a pot of coffee at her parent's house before leaving, and on the way to the office, she realized she'd left her vegan granola bars, too.

Mrs. Klingensmith took her seat behind the front desk and adjusted her glasses on her face. "Anything else I can do for you right now?" She raised her eyes to Marley's.

Marley stepped closer to the top hutch of the desk, which rose above the main surface below. She rested her hands on it. "Uh, yes. What time is the first patient?"

Mrs. Klingensmith removed her glasses with one hand and flipped through a paper appointment book with the other. After stopping on a page with today's date in bold at the top, she lifted her head. "Your father still hasn't succumbed to the technological age. He insists on keeping things in paper format. Now, where did I put my readers…" She fumbled with a few things on the desk until her fingers clasped around a pair of thick-rimmed black reading glasses. "Aha! Knew they were here somewhere. I tell you, it's the most aggravating thing to need two different pairs of glasses to navigate through life. But what are you going to do?"

Marley stood a bit taller on her tiptoes and leaned over the desk. "So, the first patient is…?" She didn't want to seem impatient, but if she had time to slip out and grab a coffee, she didn't have to be talked into it.

"Oh, yes, dear, let me see here… that's right. The first patient is Mr. Talbot. Chief complaint is a cyst. 8:30 a.m." The woman removed the darker readers and placed them aside, sitting her regular wire-rim glasses back in their usual spot on her face. She smiled.

Great. No time for coffee. It would have to wait until lunch hour. "Okay, thanks, Mrs. Klingensmith. I guess I'll get settled in Dad's office. Let me know when Mr. Talbot arrives."

The woman met Marley's gaze and nodded. "Will do. Now, don't hesitate to let me know if you need anything else. I'm sorry I can't make you a cup of coffee, but your father doesn't keep a coffeemaker in the office. He says only the weak rely on a substance to give them focus and strength. He also says it's terrible for the blood pressure." With this parting word of wisdom from Marley's father, Mrs. Klingensmith returned her attention to the appointment book in front of her.

Only the weak rely on a substance to give them focus and strength? How about only the brave survives a world where they withhold crucial-to-function liquid from those saving their medical practice? Hmm? Marley's head throbbed as she plodded into her father's office.

She flicked on the light switch and entered the office, closing the heavy door behind her. The room transported her back to her childhood. Its entire essence boasted mahogany everything and complete order. A mammoth-sized wooden desk stood in the middle of the room with a wall-to-wall bookcase behind it. Books on every subject imaginable filled its shelves. To the side were two windows and on the opposite wall hung her father's medical school degree, residency certificate, and a shadow box holding a Bronze Star medal from his time in the U.S. Army. She'd asked her father several times about the award, but he always changed the subject and refused to discuss it further.

Marley sauntered to the desk and sank into the chair, inhaling the fragrance of dust mixed with lingering scent of her father's All Spice cologne. The scene of boarding the school bus with all the neighborhood children teasing her raced through her mind again. *God, help me make it through the next few weeks. It feels like I never left, and I'm back to being the old Marley.* She didn't have time to give it further consideration because a knock wrapped on her door.

Raising her head, she found Mrs. Klingensmith standing in the doorway.

"Marley, Dear, oh, I mean, Dr. Bakersfield…that sounds strange doesn't it? But then, I guess you are Dr. Bakersfield now, um, your first patient is here. Would you like me to have him take a seat in the waiting room or place him in the exam room?"

"Thanks, Mrs. Klingensmith. The exam room will be fine. Tell him I'll be with him in a few minutes."

The woman gave a small nod and closed the door behind her.

Marley glanced to the side, looking out the window, and tapped her fingers on the desk. *Well, Dr. Bakersfield, time to go.* She whispered one more quick prayer for guidance and help and rose from her seat, ready to face her first patient in Blackstone Haven as the new, improved Dr. Bakersfield.

~

Marley whizzed through her morning, seeing mostly straightforward complaints. Flying high, she felt somewhat confident about how the next month or so would go when her stomach growled so loud that it caused Mrs. Klingensmith to lift her head from her work and pause.

"Dear, you need to get something in you. I have a snack cake if you would like it?"

Shaking her head, Marley crossed the floor to her father's office. She picked up her bag and hoisted it on her shoulder before returning. "No, thanks, Mrs. Klingensmith. I'm going to run out and grab something to eat. I'll be back before the one o'clock patient, though. Call me if there's an emergency. The hospital has my number, too."

Marley hurried to her car and drove the three streets over to Main Street, where all the local restaurants, shops, and coffee-hubs existed. She hadn't planned on frequenting Benjamin's bakery again, but before she knew what was happening, she'd put the car in park, hopped out, and walked across the street to his front door.

She pulled it open, and the scent of sugary goodness nearly knocked her over. Although she didn't like the idea of consuming non-vegan loads of sugar, her salivary glands betrayed her, and her mouth began to water.

Benjamin stood behind the counter wiping it down with a rag. As the door closed behind her with a thud, he lifted his head from his work. "Hey, Marley. It's good to see you again." He broke into a wide grin.

She walked to the counter and felt her pulse quicken. She sent him a smile and smoothed her bangs over her forehead, hoping he didn't notice her scar. "Hi, Benjamin." She scanned the half-empty bakery case below and found his eyes again. "Busy day?"

He sat his rag down and rested his forearms on the counter, leaning closer to Marley. "Yeah, they cleaned me out during the morning rush. Then, a sales rep came in an hour ago and bought every cinnamon roll I had for a business luncheon he was hosting." He stared deeper into her eyes.

She clutched the handle of her purse tighter, and her palms began to sweat. He made her nervous...in a good way. But she didn't have time for romance. She had a career to get back to D.C. And for a small town, she'd remained fairly busy all morning seeing patients at her father's practice. Plus, she didn't like the idea of letting someone get close to her--of seeing her. Look how that had gone during her childhood. *Terrible.* She'd been teased, ridiculed, mocked. No, life held less pain if she only relied on herself and didn't let others into her circle. She had Tara—that was enough.

He leaned a bit closer and lowered his voice. "What's going on in that head of yours? You look like you're thinking awfully hard."

Clearing her throat, Marley stood straighter and changed the subject. "Oh, nothing. I'm wondering how great those cinnamon rolls must have been to get totally snatched up."

"Well, why don't you find out for yourself. I've got a batch in the oven, and they're almost done. Give me two minutes."

Before Marley could object, he'd spun around and grabbed a towel. He opened the oven door and laid it flat. Bending down her reached forward to grab the tray off the bottom rack, but instead of standing upright with a sheet filled with baked goodness, he screamed, "Ouch. I can't believe I did that."

Marley furrowed her brow. "What? What did you do?"

He turned around, facing her, and covered his arm with the towel. Sweat beaded across his forehead, and he grimaced. "I burned my arm on the edge of the rack. I don't know what I was thinking. I've pulled stuff out of there a million times...I must have been distracted." He sent her a pained but flirtatious smile.

Marley's face warmed, but she shifted into doctor mode and rattled off a series of orders and questions, "Run it under cool or cold water. Is it numb, or does it hurt? Can I take a look at it? Do you have any silver sulfadiazine cream?"

He obeyed Marley's orders and headed to the sink on the left side of the oven and turned on the cold water.

Marley opened the swinging door to the right of the checkout area and stepped behind the counter. She walked over to Benjamin to inspect his injury. Reaching for his forearm, she took his hand in hers. "Here, let me have a look." She examined it and determined the burn not to be too deep. "It's not as bad as it could have been, but I think you should stop by my office later today and let me put a real dressing on it."

He locked eyes with her, his hand still clasped in hers. With a soft voice, he agreed, "I'll do that. I don't think I have any of the silver sulfa-what's-its-name in my bakery. Besides, I don't mind the idea of seeing my doctor again."

Marley suspected her face had turned beet red at this point after his flattery. Not that she objected to it. Quite the opposite. Although his interest made her uneasy in some respects, it also excited her. She looked down at his forearm and realized his hand remained in hers. "Oh, I'm sorry." She dropped it and flicked her eyes away.

He reached for her hand again and grabbed it. "I'm not."

The front door to the bakery opened, announcing another visitor. Realizing she and Benjamin had an audience, Marley jumped away. "Well, make sure you come to see me, and I'll take care of that arm. Keep it covered until then." She hurried out of the bakery so fast she didn't realize she'd forgotten to get any food or drink until she made it to her car.

Digging in the glove compartment for two minutes rewarded her with a crumpled vegan granola bar and a box of breath mints Tara must have left there during their last outing. She wolfed down the mushed bar and sped back to her father's practice, her hands shaking as she drove.

Benjamin's words echoed in her ear, "I'm not."

He didn't seem sorry she'd held his hand, and if she was honest with herself, neither was she. The thought of seeing him in a few hours caused her stomach to toss like a gymnast doing flips. No, she wasn't sorry about it at all.

Chapter 10

December 16, 2019, Monday

Benjamin drove his car to Marley's office. The closer he got to his destination, the faster his heart beat, which made his arm throb more. He winced, marveling at the pain a few seconds-worth of searing could inflict. He had a new respect for his oven.

Pulling into one of the open parking spaces in the gravel lot, he drew in a deep breath. As he turned off the ignition, he noticed his palms had dampened. *Why was he so nervous?* Because he liked Marley…a lot… he'd always liked her, even when they were children riding their bikes around the neighborhood. He could imagine the dusting of freckles across her pale cheeks and the sun creating beams of honey off her copper locks. Her intelligence impressed him. She didn't behave in a silly manner like the other girls his age, always batting their eyelashes and trying to call him on the phone.

A horn honk startled him, and he turned his head toward the sound to see what had caused it. He wasn't even driving, so he didn't see how he could be to blame.

Marley's mother waved from the car beside him and smiled.

Since he was a child, he'd known Marley's parents, and they still attended the same church as him, Faith Community Church. Basically, everyone in the town went there, and in a town the size of Blackstone Haven, everybody knew everybody. *And everybody's business.*

She hopped out of her car and walked over to his, waiting for him to exit it.

Turning off the ignition and setting the parking brake, Benjamin slid out and grinned. "Mrs. Bakersfield, it's good to see you. Are you meeting Marley?" Wearing a pink flowing top and jeans, she looked like the epitome of maternal goodness.

Patting her hair, she nodded and grinned. "Yes. I hope she'll be glad to see me. I didn't tell her I was stopping by, and she often hates interruptions when she's working, but I made her some honeybuns and wanted to bring them while they're hot."

"That sounds delicious. I'm sure she'll appreciate it. I can't imagine she wouldn't want to see you. You're one of the kindest women in this town." He gestured ahead with his hand. "After you."

"Thank you, Benjamin. I hope you're right and she won't be upset. These honeybuns were her favorite treat when she was little. Her father and I appreciate her help during this time, and I wanted to do something for her. Plus, she's gotten too thin. All skin and bones. Have you seen her?" She had been walking ahead of him and stopped, turning around.

He raised his injured arm in the air as proof. "Yeah. Marley stopped in my bakery earlier today and offered to take care of my arm. I burned it on the oven. We didn't have a lot of time to catch up, though." He took the stairs to the office's front door and opened it for Mrs. Bakersfield.

She gave him a grin and patted his non-injured arm as she passed through. "Thank you, Dear. You always were such a sweet boy. Your mother would be proud of you...and what you've done with the bakery. Such a shame you had to give up that job in New York, though."

Benjamin's stomach clenched in the way it did every time someone mentioned his mother. Even though she'd passed away several years ago, the pain still felt fresh. He didn't like to think about it--what he'd lost. He closed the door to the medical office behind them and turned Mrs. Bakersfield's attention to Marley, who stood ten feet away looking like a model from a print ad. She'd let her long, wavy locks loose, and they settled down her back like a crimson waterfall.

She lifted her head and took in the sight of her mother holding a tray of baked goods and Benjamin in her entryway. Her eye's widened. "Mom, hey. What are you doing here? I didn't know you were coming by," she spoke to her mother, but the entire time kept her eyes fixed on Benjamin's face.

Mrs. Bakersfield carried the tray to Marley and sat it on the front desk's hutch. "I'm sorry to drop in like this, Honeybun, but I wanted to make sure you had something to eat. And to see how your first day was going."

Marley made a tiny cringe when her mother called her Honeybun, but if he hadn't been staring at her, taking in all her beauty, he wouldn't have noticed it.

"I'm good, Mom. I think the day has gone well. I've been busy, but that's how I like it."

Benjamin walked closer to the two Bakersfield women.

Marley's face turned a deep red shade.

"Honeybun, are you feeling okay? You look flushed." Marley's mother put the back of her hand on her daughter's forehead. "You don't have a fever, do you?" Her mother's brow crinkled.

Pushing the hand away from her face, Marley shook her head. "No, Mom, I don't have a fever. I think it's hot in here." She turned to the secretary behind the desk, who wore a bemused expression as she took in the impromptu afternoon drama. "Mrs. Klingensmith, could you turn the thermostat down, please?"

Mrs. Klingensmith rose from her seat behind the desk and gave a small nod. "No problem. I'll turn it down and go get the exam room ready for your next patient. It looks like our town baker needs some attention. Mrs. Bakersfield, it was good seeing you again." The secretary walked to the exam room, chuckling as she left.

Marley's mother didn't seem to notice the awkward silence that followed but instead busied herself digging through her purse for something. "Aha, I knew I had some in here." She shoved a small, white bottle in Marley's hands, and it made a rattling sound.

Marley lifted the bottle to inspect the lettering. "Aspirin?"

Her mother bobbed her head. "Yes, for your fever. Now, I'm going to get out of your way. Benjamin said you had an appointment with him but promise me you'll take two of those." She turned to leave but paused. "Oh, and maybe you shouldn't see anyone else after him today. What with your temperature and all? Your father wouldn't want you to infect the entire town. How would that look?" She walked to the door and blew Marley a kiss before exiting. "See you at home, Honeybun. I'll have a nice supper ready for you. Maybe some chicken noodle soup would be good."

Sighing, Marley placed the aspirin on the desk and raised her eyes to meet Benjamin's. "I'm sorry about that. And I'm not sick."

He sent her a half-grin and shrugged. "No worries. I didn't think you were. Your mom meant well. At least you still have her. That's a blessing."

Marley reached out a hand and placed it on Benjamin's shoulder. "I'm sorry. I wasn't thinking. I forgot about your mom…I mean…I didn't forget, but sometimes I…I apologize. None of that came out the right way. Please forgive me."

He shook his head and locked eyes with Marley. He could lose himself in the emerald pools. "Nothing to apologize about…I understand. So…I guess you should take a look at this arm." He raised the bandaged forearm.

She grinned. "Yes, let's get you taken care of so you can get back to baking. Follow me." She led him to the exam room, where Mrs. Klingensmith had entered a few minutes prior.

On the way in, Mrs. Klingensmith passed them and sent Benjamin a knowing look.

Marley patted the top of the exam table. "Okay, have a seat here." She turned around and gathered supplies from the counter behind her.

He watched as she pulled out bandages, gauze, and a tub of ointment. As she assembled the materials, he couldn't help but notice how gracefully she moved.

As if she could sense his eyes upon her, Marley peered over her shoulder and found his gaze, blushing again. "I've got everything ready now. Let me take a look at that burn. Did you leave it covered all day like I advised?" Her brow arched, and she got to work removing the makeshift dressing she'd created for him earlier.

The gentle touch of her fingertips as they grazed his skin sent a jolt through him. He tried to act calm and responded with a brief, "Absolutely. I followed the doctor's orders."

She lifted her eyes from her work and found his. Smiling, she said, "Good," and then returned to her task.

Ten minutes later, Marley had cleaned his wound with saline, applied ointment, and redressed the site. He winced a few times as she finished.

Marley paused at his wince and placed her hand tenderly on his forearm next to the wound. "Are you okay? I'm sorry if it hurts. I'm all done, and each day it should feel a little better."

With her hand resting on his arm, he couldn't think of the pain, only her touch. He didn't want her to move. He wanted them to stay like this forever. He gazed into her eyes and saw the warmth and kindness he'd known all his life. Swallowing, he paused before answering, "It feels better already."

A strand of hair fell in front of Marley's eyes.

He reached forward and, with his free hand, brushed it away, tucking it behind her ear.

She stared at him, and the room fell silent.

He felt himself drawn to her and his face inched closer to hers.

Mrs. Klingensmith burst through the closed exam room door. "I wanted to see if I could get you anything before I leave." She took in the scene in front of her--Marley and Benjamin in an almost-kiss--and sputtered, "Oh, I'm sorry. I didn't mean to... I'll go. Dear, if you need anything, give me a call. Otherwise, I'll see you tomorrow." In a flash, Mrs. Klingensmith had ducked around the door.

Marley's head snapped back. "Mrs. Klingensmith! It's not what it looks like...Mrs. Klingensmith."

Benjamin started chuckling.

Marley tapped him on his non-injured arm. "It's not funny. I know she is a Sunday school teacher, but she's also one of the biggest town gossips. She'll have it broadcast across Blackstone Haven by morning that you and I are engaged."

Shrugging, Benjamin thought it wouldn't be the worst thing he could imagine. "Hey, you can't worry too much about what other people think. Other people are usually wrong, anyway. Besides, the way the rumor mill operates around here, it'll be old news by tomorrow night. Someone else is sure to do something more scandalous."

"You're probably right." She turned away from him and started cleaning up her mess. With her back to him, she gave him instructions, "You're all set. Make sure you change the dressing at least once a day. I'll put some things you'll need in a bag for you to take home. Oh, and I'll write you a script for the ointment. I don't have any extra to give to you, but the pharmacy should be able to get it for you." Marley placed extra gauze and wraps in a white paper bag and folded the top over before turning and handing it to him. "Any questions?"

He took her offering and smiled. "Yeah, I do have a question. What are you doing this weekend?"

She shrugged. "Nothing other than being on call 24/7 for the practice. Why?"

Benjamin took a deep breath and pressed ahead. "How do you feel about walnut farms?"

Raising a quizzical brow, Marley inquired, "Walnut farms? I don't know anything about them, but I like walnuts. Why?"

Benjamin nodded. "The Chamber of Commerce is hosting its annual bake-off competition for charity on New Year's Eve. This weekend is the last chance I'll have a chunk of time to prepare for it. I could use a hand." He waved his maimed arm again. "What with being injured and all."

Marley opened her mouth and then closed it.

He watched as she considered her answer, not knowing the cause of her hesitation. "Please?" He lifted his forehead and pressed his hands together in a pleading gesture.

She broke into a grin. "You wore me down. I'm in. Where do you want me to meet you and what time?"

Sliding off the exam table, Benjamin closed the space between them. "Don't worry about it. I'll pick you up at your parent's house on Saturday…say around noon?"

Nodding, she agreed, "Perfect. It'll give me time to round on any hospital patients in the morning. What do I wear to this farm?"

"You mean you've never been to my aunt's farm when you were a kid?"

She shook her head. "No. I spent most of my weekends as a kid in my bedroom studying." She walked out of the exam room, flicking the light switch on the way out the door.

Benjamin followed her lead. He walked beside her to the front door. "I'd wear some waterproof boots in case it rains or snows. You never know this time of year…and a heavy coat. Gloves, a hat. Things to keep you warm in case we spend a lot of time outside. That's about it." He glanced at her heels and smiled. "Definitely not those."

She gave him a playful nudge on the shoulder, guiding him out the door. "Yeah, yeah. No heels. I got it. Okay, I'll be ready. Saturday at noon."

"See you then." He walked out the door but glanced over his shoulder one last time. "Hey, Marley."

She stood in the doorway, one hand holding the door open, the other resting against the frame. Tilting her head, she sent him a smile that made his heart race. "Yeah."

"Thanks for taking care of me. I'm glad you're home."

Her cheeks tinged pink. "No problem…and me, too. I wasn't looking forward to coming back home, but it's turning out…alright. More than alright."

He raised his good arm in a wave and grinned. "See you Saturday."

She shut the door.

Benjamin walked to his car and got in, but instead of starting it, he sat still, reviewing the afternoon's events. After his mom passed away, he hadn't wanted to come home, either. He'd had plans. Big plans. And in the years since her death, he'd often wondered why he'd stayed in Blackstone Haven. *Maybe Marley was why. Maybe God had a plan.* As he turned this thought over in his mind, he started the car. The engine roared to life and echoed the fire that had started burning in his heart for the girl he'd loved since he was a kid on a bike, defending her honor to the neighborhood bullies. *Yeah, things were definitely more than alright…and Saturday couldn't come soon enough.*

Chapter 11

December 21, 2019, Saturday

Marley's week passed in a blur of excisions, surgical consults, and full days of clinic. She'd finally met Mrs. Klingensmith's granddaughter, Corkie, yesterday and instantly felt a connection to the teen.

Corkie had walked into the clinic after school on Friday. She'd planned to swing by earlier in the week but had begged off to study for a test. She opened the door and crept inside.

Marley didn't notice her standing next to her in front of the desk.

"Corkie, dear, I didn't know you were coming by today. How did your exam go?" Mrs. Klingensmith popped out of the exam room she'd been tidying and hurried to her granddaughter, scooping her into a bear hug.

Marley had been scribbling a note to herself at the front desk and raised her head at Mrs. Klingensmith's jubilation. She waited until the grandmother released her granddaughter to introduce herself, "Hi, I'm Dr. Bakersfield. Well, the younger Dr. Bakersfield. The real Dr. Bakersfield is my dad, but he's at home resting, so I'm the current Dr. Bakersfield." She stuck her hand out, ready to shake the teenager's hand.

The girl ducked her head down and stared at her feet, muttering, "Hi."

"Now, dear, don't be shy." Mrs. Klingensmith tapped her granddaughter on the arm. She raised her eyes to Marley's and explained, "She's a quiet girl, but smart as a whip. I'm so proud of her. She had an Anatomy test today, and I bet she aced it." Turning her attention to Corkie once again, she gave her another encouraging tap on the arm. "Go on, then, tell us how you did. Don't leave us hanging."

The girl lifted her head and gave Marley a meek smile. "I got a 100. Only one in my class."

"Wow, that's amazing. You must like Anatomy. Is it your favorite subject?"

"Oh, she likes all things school-related...anything academic, really. She wants to be a doctor one day. Don't you, Corkie?" Mrs. Klingensmith nudged her granddaughter in the side with her elbow.

"Grandma..." Corkie protested at the bragging.

"Well, it's true. And she's going to do it, too. Never seen anything she set her mind to that she didn't achieve." Mrs. Klingensmith looked at Corkie closer. "Dear, you have something stuck to the back of your shirt." The woman fiddled with a piece of paper and picked it off, reading it. "Dorky Corkie...Corkie, who did this?" Mrs. Klingensmith's lips tightened.

Corkie grabbed the sticky note from her grandmother and shoved it in the front pocket of her jeans. Mumbling, she darted her eyes to the floor again, "It's nothing, Grandma...just some kids goofing around."

"I don't think it's funny. Does your mother know about this? Do you want me to call your principal?" Mrs. Klingensmith's cheeks flamed.

"No, Grandma, I'll handle it. I'm used to it."

"Was it that Blackstone girl again? I'm going to call Mr. Blackstone and give him a piece of my mind. Because he owns almost everything in the town, he thinks his family owns everyone in it, too. Well, I won't stand for it. I—"

Corkie spoke louder, "Grandma, stop. Please don't make it worse than it already is, okay? I want to get through high school and get out of here... that's all."

Marley understood exactly how Corkie felt. She'd uttered those same words to her own mother after an unfortunate incident with Stacey Blackstone at the Homecoming dance in twelfth grade. "Mrs. Klingensmith, it's getting late. Perhaps, you'd like to head home early? I can finish up here on my own."

The woman raised a brow. "Are you sure, dear? Is there anything you need before I go?"

Marley glanced at the teenager whose shoulders relaxed and looked relieved at the opportunity to distract her grandmother from the current conversation. "Actually, would you mind checking the exam room for my doctor bag? The little black one I carry with me on the weekends. I think I may have shoved it in a drawer, and I might need it for rounds tomorrow."

Mrs. Klingensmith nodded. "Not a problem. Be right back. Corkie, are you riding home with me?"

She cast a look at her grandmother and patted her jean pocket, now hiding away the offensive note. "Uh, actually grandma, I think I'll walk home. It's good exercise, and it's only a few blocks. But thanks."

"Anytime, dear." Her grandmother hurried to the exam room, leaving Corkie and Marley alone at the front desk.

Marley cleared her throat. "So, the kids at school give you a hard time?" She lifted her forehead.

Corkie stared at the ground but remained silent. She shrugged.

"You know, I got teased a lot growing up here. A lot. It was horrible. So much so, I didn't want to come back here ever again. But," she spread her hands wide, "here I am. My dad called, duty called, and I'm back where I promised myself, I'd never return."

Corkie met Marley's eyes finally. "People bullied you?" Her mouth dropped as if the concept seemed impossible.

Nodding her head, Marley continued, "Yep. Stacey Blackstone mainly, but a few of her followers joined in on the tormenting…from before the time I could ride a bike until I left this town."

"I can't imagine anyone picking on you… you're beautiful and smart."

Marley still didn't feel beautiful, but she wasn't going to argue with the girl while trying to convince her that things would get better. "You're beautiful and smart, too, Corkie. Can you talk to anyone at school about the bullying? A teacher, your principal…someone?"

Corkie shook her head.

"Who is this girl that's giving you a hard time? You said she's a Blackstone? Any relation to Stacey?"

"Her name's Chelsea. Chelsea Blackstone. She's pretty, tall, blond, and smart enough. I usually beat her on exams, though, and it makes her mad. She's Stacey Blackstone's niece. So, it wouldn't matter if I told anyone...with her being a Blackstone, nobody would do anything about it."

Marley stepped forward and put a hand on Corkie's shoulder. She glanced toward the exam room, but thankfully Mrs. Klingensmith was taking her time finding the bag. "Promise me something."

"What?"

"If you need help...if things get worse, or you feel down... you'll let me know? Or someone?"

The girl cracked her first genuine smile of the evening. "Okay. Dr. Bakersfield?"

"Yeah?"

"Do you think I could shadow you sometime? Maybe a few days a week after school? For a few hours. I do want to become a physician one day. I read in my college application book that pre-med programs like to see volunteer and shadowing hours." The young girl stared at Marley with pleading eyes.

The last thing Marley needed right now was another distraction—someone to get underfoot. But she couldn't help it. The girl tugged at Marley's heart, and she saw so much of herself in the young girl. Before she knew what had happened, the words tumbled out, "Sure. Meet me here next Monday and bring a pen and paper."

Mrs. Klingensmith returned with Marley's bag, placing it on the desk. "Here you go. Have a good evening, Dr. Bakersfield. Ready to go, Corkie? You sure you don't want to ride home with me? I promise to drop all the school business. We can sing along to Christmas Carols in the car." She shrugged into her heavy wool coat.

Corkie peered at her grandmother's outerwear and glanced toward the door. "Maybe I will go with you, grandma. It's getting cold outside." Sending her grandmother an appreciative smile, she grabbed her backpack off the floor and slipped into her jacket.

Marley reached for a stack of papers off the desk and picked up her purse and the medical bag Mrs. Klingensmith had found for her. She tucked the sheets inside her purse and followed the duo to the door. Before flicking the lights off for the night, Marley's hand paused. She stuck her head out the door and called to the departing girl, "Hey."

Corkie had walked out the door and started down the stairs. She stopped at the bottom step and turned. "Yeah," Corkie asked, shivering in the crisp winter air. She's pulled a hat and gloves out of her backpack and put them.

Marley set her gaze upon the young girl's face. "I meant what I said before. If you need anything…"

The girl rubbed the arms of her down jacket with her gloved hands. "Thanks, Dr. Bakersfield. See you Monday."

Marley waved goodbye and then locked the door. When she turned around again, the girl and her grandmother had gone. "See you Monday," Marley whispered to the wind.

Chapter 12

December 21, 2019, Saturday

Thinking back to the conversation the day prior with Corkie, Marley couldn't help but think how much the teenager reminded her of herself as a young girl. Not that the two of them physically resembled one another. Corkie had lean, long legs and gorgeous, wavy chestnut hair. By contrast, Marley couldn't recall a time in her younger eighteen years when she hadn't favored a frizzy head tethered to a lumpy, pale body below. Add in a short period of braces and intermittent acne episodes, and Marley thought Corkie had it pretty good.

Something about the way Corkie carried herself made it apparent she didn't realize her own outward beauty. It seemed her confidence had yet to develop…well, Marley identified with that feeling. She'd found herself clamping her mouth shut so as not to yell, "Hey kid, you've got a lot going for you. Don't get down on yourself. Chin up, smile, you're great."

Marley shook her head, willing her thoughts back to the present. Her heart rate increased as she thought about her upcoming date with Benjamin. Peering at the clock on the wall, she realized he'd be here any minute. Marley stepped in front of the oval mirror by her parent's front door, checking to see if her scar was visible. After a quick smoothing of her bangs, she felt reasonably satisfied with the result. Not perfect, but as good as it was going to get right now.

A knock on the door caused Marley to shift her eyes away from her reflection. She opened the door, and her heart beat faster. "Hi, Benjamin."

He stood before her, resting one muscular arm against the doorframe. He wore a grey cable knit sweater and dark wash jeans. His jet-black hair made his blue eyes appear almost aquamarine today. "Hey, Marley. You look…amazing. Are you ready to go?"

His gaze and compliment caused her knees to weaken. She was ready to go but not confident her feet would work.

He grinned, waiting for a response.

"Um, yeah. I'm ready. Let me grab my purse and lock the door." Somehow finding the strength to move, Marley bent down and lifted her bag off the floor. After slinging it on her shoulder, she locked the front door and turned around to face Benjamin again. "Ready."

"After you." He gestured with his hands for her to walk ahead of him to his car.

She obliged, and he followed behind her.

He opened the door for her, and she slid inside. Shutting her door for her, he went to the opposite side of the car and took his seat, too.

Acutely aware of his proximity, Marley's foot started tapping against the floor mat, creating a tap-tap sound. She tried to settle her leg and stop the distraction by placing a hand on her knee. It worked--for a few seconds. Stop it. Pull it together. It's Benjamin. Little Bennie Miller. From school. Besides, he probably isn't interested in anything more than friendship.

Benjamin started the car, but before putting it into drive, he caught Marley's eye. "I'm glad you agreed to come with me today. I—" He stopped speaking, as if debating whether to say the next words, "I'm looking forward to spending time with you."

A flutter began in Marley's chest and rose upward. She swallowed. Benjamin was excited to spend time with her. And he thought she looked amazing. "Me, too. Thanks for inviting me."

His grin widened. "I can't wait for you to see the farm. It's old, but I love it there." He shoved the car into gear and took off down the road.

Twenty minutes later, the car pulled up a graveled driveway in front of a large red barn and a worn, but charming, white farmhouse. The farmhouse boasted a wrap-around porch and stood at least two stories tall. The barn doors remained closed, and white fencing surrounded the property. Beyond the barn, a few horses wearing cozy blankets across their backs speckled a big field.

Marley stepped out of the car, and her mouth fell. She glanced towards Benjamin across the hood of the vehicle. "Is this all yours?"

He shrugged his shoulders and his neck flushed red. "Yeah. After my aunt passed, and then a year later, my mom, I inherited it." He started walking to the main house, his hands shoved in his front pockets.

"I didn't realize this property belonged to your family. My dad used to drive my mom and me past it when I was a child. It's fantastic."

He led the way to the front door, holding it open for her. "Thanks. It's peaceful here. And wait until you see the kitchen—a baker's dream."

Marley smiled and stepped into the entryway. White plankboard lined the living room walls and the hallway leading toward the kitchen. Overhead exposed wooden beams gave a rustic feel to the space. The aroma of pine mixed with cinnamon welcomed her and made her feel at home. She inhaled again. "Do you have a real Christmas tree?"

"Is there any other type?"

"My family always used an artificial one. With my dad's schedule, we never knew when we'd get a chance to take it down and dispose of it, so if we'd used a real one, it might have rotted through February. Or longer."

"That's a shame. Everyone should have a real Christmas tree. It's one of the best things about Christmas." He gave her a warm smile and nodded toward the couch. "You can toss your coat and bag there and follow me."

As she slipped past him to place her belongings down, her hand grazed his. The tips of her fingers tingled, and her face felt flush. She tried to change the subject and hoped he didn't notice the heat in her cheeks. "So, I guess we better get started if we're going to get a trial run for the bake-off done before the evening is over."

He nodded. "Right. Follow me." He headed down the hallway to the white and stainless-steel kitchen. Marley suspected she could fit her car inside the stove. "Wow, this is impressive."

"Thanks. My aunt loved to cook, so this was the one room she kept updated. I spent the summer painting the barn and repairing fencing, but the house still needs a lot of work. Benjamin made his way to the refrigerator and pulled out a series of ingredients. He placed eggs, milk, and butter on the counter and then proceeded toward a thin cabinet to the left of the stove and removed several spices and sugar. Turning to her, his gaze lingered for a moment.

"Can I help you?"

He spun around and dug in a drawer, handing her an embroidered white and red apron. "Here, put this on, so you don't ruin your clothes."

She took the apron from his hand and ran her fingers over the intricate design sewed on the front of the apron. "It's pretty."

"It belonged to my mother." He didn't raise his head to meet her eyes but instead busied himself with setting bowls, utensils, and pans on the counter. She saw him fiddle with a knob on the oven, his back still facing away from her.

"Oh," Marley uttered, wanting to kick herself for not realizing it sooner.

"It's okay. I'm glad to see someone using it again. Especially since I've decided what to make for the competition."

Marley tied the apron around her waist and neck and stepped up to the counter next to him. "Alright, the suspense is killing me. What are we making?"

"Cinnamon rolls."

"Don't you make cinnamon rolls every day at the bakery? Not that they aren't great—they are—but won't people expect something different?"

He raised a finger in the air. "Ah, but these won't be ordinary cinnamon rolls. These will be my mother's secret recipe with a twist. A Benjamin and Marley twist."

Noticing how close they stood, Marley's heart pounded faster. "A Benjamin and Marley twist?"

He lowered his face to hers, only inches between their lips. Benjamin whispered, "Exactly. It will take everyone by surprise."

Marley closed her eyes, letting her guard down. She lifted her lips toward his, but the oven timer blared, "Beep beep. Beep beep. Beep beep." Startled, Marley's eyes flew wide open. "What was that?"

Benjamin wore a sheepish grin and chuckled. "Sorry. I set the preheat timer on the oven."

"Preheat, huh? I've heard of that… I can't say I've ever used it myself. My motto is to throw the food in and turn the oven on, then hope for the best. Or skip cooking altogether and get takeout."

Benjamin's grin widened, and he took a step back. "Come on. Let me show you what to do." He pulled a white stand mixer forward and lifted the top of it. Mixing together yeast and warm water, he set it aside for a few minutes before adding the remainder of the ingredients into a mixing bowl.

Attaching a curved hook to the top of the mixer, Benjamin lowered it into the bowl.

Marley pointed at the hook-like object. "What's that?"

He glanced over at her and smiled. "It's a bread hook. Haven't you made bread before?"

She arched a brow and cocked her head. "Again, the takeout, remember?"

Placing a hand on top of the mixer, Benjamin gave a slight nod. "Right." He turned on the machine and after a few minutes of mixing, removed the dough. Carrying it to the island in the middle of the kitchen, Benjamin spread it out on the counter he'd sprinkled with flour while the dough churned. He looked at Marley and waved for her to move closer to the island. "Come stand here."

She stepped in front of the dough on one side of the island.

Benjamin moved closer to her. "Give it a go." He nodded toward the dough.

She placed her hands into the gooey mixture and pushed on it. "Am I doing this right?" She lifted her head and flicked her eyes to him.

He reached for the dough, his hands brushing hers as he showed her how to work the dough. "Knead your hands in the dough like this." Benjamin placed his hands on hers and guided them through the mixture.

A shiver traveled down her spine. She didn't know how he managed to do it, but Benjamin Miller made her feel like the most beautiful woman on earth.

After several minutes of toe-curling mixing, Marley found her voice again, "Um, how do we know when it's ready?"

"When you know, you know. It takes time, patience, and a little love."

She didn't know if his reference pertained to the bread dough or their budding relationship. Staring at his strong arms, she imagined them encircling her in his sure, steady embrace. At the same time, she knew she had to leave and return to the real world soon. What then? She'd get to spend enough time with him to fall in love, only to have him break her heart.

Marley gave herself a shake. "So, now what do we do?"

Still standing beside her, Benjamin answered her question with one of his own, "About?"

About us, she wanted to shout but instead inquired, "About the rolls. What's the next step?"

Benjamin gave her a grin and stepped away from the counter. "Now we wait. We have to let the bread dough rise for at least an hour. I thought you might be hungry, so I made you a salad."

She sent him a relieved smile. "That sounds great. I am starving." She followed him to a wooden table next to the kitchen wall and took a seat.

He sat next to her and offered his hand to hers before bowing his head.

She followed suit and closed her eyes.

"Father, thank you for this time together and for the blessing of rekindled friendships. Thank you for this food and for the company of this wonderful woman. Please bless our evening together and help us develop a winning recipe. Amen."

Marley laughed as she raised her head. "You prayed to win the competition?"

Shrugging, Benjamin dug into his food. "Hey, God tells us to bring all our requests to Him. To ask Him for what we need and to thank Him for what He has done. So that's what I did."

He smiled. "Besides, my intentions are good. I want to win, sure. I want the bragging rights and to get the prize money to help the bakery, but I also want to raise a lot of money for the hospital. The Lord looks at the heart, right?"

Chewing in silence, Marley considered this. Ask God for what she needed? What did she need? To see herself the way He saw her; the way Benjamin saw her? To let someone into her heart? To accept herself as God made her?

Benjamin swallowed and set his fork down. "You're quiet. Everything okay?"

Tears filled her eyes, and Marley chastised herself. Do not cry. Not in front of him. That's one thing her father always told her—never let anyone see your weakness. Those were the words he'd shared with her the day she came home after the infamous bike wreck, and they haunted her still today. "I'm fine."

"You're not fine."

A tear trailed down her cheek, and she wiped it away with her finger. "Well, I'm not fine. But… it's…oh, it's everything, I suppose. It's my dad getting hurt and my relationship with my parents. Mainly, it's still feeling like that kid who crashed her bike all those years ago. Returning to Blackstone Haven…well, I didn't realize the feelings it would resurrect."

He stared at her for a second before responding, "Me either. Marley, I like—"

"Beep beep, beep beep, beep beep." Clamping his mouth shut, Benjamin jumped up from the table and rushed to the oven. He hit the timer button, silencing it, and turned around facing Marley. "Ready for phase two?"

She smiled and stood. "Sure, what's phase two?"

"The dough should be finished rising, so now we have to roll it out and add our secret ingredient." He wagged his eyebrows.

Marley raised a brow. "Which is?"

Benjamin headed to the pantry on the opposite side of the kitchen and returned, wielding a mason jar filled with something. "This."

Marley scrunched her forehead. "What is it?"

"Walnuts. Black walnuts, to be exact. Fresh from the Miller Farm." He displayed a proud grin.

"So, we roll out some dough and add the walnuts, and that's it? We're finished?"

"Almost. I gathered some apples this fall from the orchard, too, and canned them, so they're ready to add to the rolls. After that, we'll slice everything into circular pieces, bake them in the oven, and then add the best part."

"What's the best part?"

"My mother's cream cheese icing. No one else in the tri-state area makes it better. She used my grandmother's recipe. It's been in my family forever."

"That sounds delicious. Sugary, but delicious."

"Trust me, it's going to smell so good that even you will have a taste. It's irresistible." He waved for her to join him at the counter and showed her how to add the walnuts and apples to the dough. Then, he cut them into even sections. Slipping them in the oven, Benjamin shared with Marley about his time in New York.

"It sounds wonderful. Do you ever think about going back one day?"

"Sometimes. When my mom got sick, I did what I had to do. I came home to cover the bakery and keep it running and to care for her. Then, when she passed and left me the house and this land, I thought I'd stick around for a while. See what I could build here. Plus, the idea of selling the bakery or closing it didn't seem right. It's the last piece of my mom. I do miss the idea of building something bigger, though. I had major plans for the restaurant in New York."

"And you were the French pastry chef there?"

"Yeah, for all of about a month. But God had different plans. That's the thing—you never know what the future holds. Or the past." He stared intently at Marley.

She gazed into his eyes for a few seconds before glancing away. "Yeah, you never know. Although I can tell you, the past usually holds a lot of pain." She shifted her weight and fiddled with the ends of her hair. "But enough of that talk."

"How's your dad doing?"

"He's doing well. Stubborn, of course, but I think his leg is healing well. His physician seems pleased. Dad riddles me with a million questions when I get home from the clinic each day. I usually spend an hour assuring him that the place won't spontaneously combust in his absence. Other than that, he's good."

"And your mom?"

"She's fine. Driving me crazy trying to fill me with every known baked item on the planet, but fine. We've had our moments since I came home, but I think we are both trying to understand one another better."

"So, what about your practice in D.C.? When do you have to return?"

Marley walked across the kitchen to the sink and kept her back to Benjamin. Trying to change the subject, she inquired, "Could I get a glass of water?" She didn't want to think about leaving Benjamin. Marley couldn't say the same for Blackstone Haven, but she'd miss him terribly when she left.

"Sure." He stepped next to her and reached overhead to get a glass from the cabinet. As he handed it to her, he brushed her cheek with the other hand.

She flinched; afraid he'd uncover her scar.

He shook his head and smoothed his fingers across her forehead, tracing the path of her scar. "You don't have to do that—to hide. You don't have to hide anything about yourself. You're beautiful, the most beautiful person I've known. Scar and all."

Marley's palms sweat, and she thought she might drop the glass he'd handed her.

Benjamin leaned down and kissed her forehead.

"Beep beep, beep beep, beep beep."

"Agh, I'm going to throw out the oven alarm. It has terrible timing." Benjamin chuckled.

"I agree." She smiled.

Benjamin walked to the oven and pulled the cinnamon rolls out, careful not to bump his arm on the edge of the hot rack.

"How's your arm doing?"

He patted the bandaged forearm below his pushed-up sleeve. "It's great. Almost healed over. Thanks to my fantastic doctor." He showed her how to mix the cream cheese icing.

Marley spread it across the top of the rolls like he'd showed her to do.

He grinned. "Now, for the best part."

"Which is?"

"Taste-testing. Every good baker tries out their creation before serving it to others. We have to see if this is competition worthy." He cut a small piece of the hot, gooey roll and handed it to Marley.

"I don't really eat sugar. Or dairy. Or anything that can decrease your life-span or add width to the hips."

"One bite of cinnamon roll won't kill you. And I don't think you need to worry about your figure."

Marley's face burned, but she accepted the morsel and popped it in her mouth. The nuts and apples complemented the cinnamon spice perfectly. The icing melted, coating the entire bite in cream cheese heaven. "This is the best thing I've ever eaten. Seriously."

"See, I told you. Good enough to win the Chamber of Commerce Bake-off on New Year's Eve?"

"For sure. No one else has a chance. Your mom would be proud."

"Thanks, Marley. So, what are your plans for Christmas and New Year's?"

"Nothing too crazy. With my dad on crutches, we're going to keep things low-key. Well, as low-key as my mom can manage. Christmas sends her into a tizzy. I'll still be on call for dad's patients, so I may have to run to the hospital, too. No plans for New Year's, though. What about you?"

"Christmas Eve will be busy at the bakery, but I close the bakery Christmas day because I like to go to the service at church."

"My mom mentioned that, so maybe I'll see you there."

"I'd like that. I'll save you a seat…I wanted to ask you a favor."

"Sure."

"Since you don't have any plans for New Year's Eve, would you be my partner in the Bake-off? I could use an extra set of hands, and now you know my secret ingredient and my mother's cream cheese icing recipe, so I've got to make sure the competition doesn't snag you."

Marley gave a small laugh. "I don't think there's any chance of that happening." She could help him, but she already liked him…a lot. If she kept spending time with him, she suspected her feelings would exponentially grow. And the knowledge that she'd be leaving in a few weeks hung heavy over her head.

He made pleading hands. "Please. I'm begging."

She took a deep breath and intended to decline his request, but instead gushed, "Sure. I'd love to help. Besides, you need a medic on hand in case you try to injure yourself again."

He shook his head. "Funny. I'll try to keep the dangerous baking to a minimum." The sky had darkened outside, and the living room held a pleasant glow from the twinkling lights on Benjamin's Christmas tree. "I can't believe how late it got. I guess I'd better take you home."

Her shoulders sagged. She hated for the evening to end. "I guess so. Otherwise, my mother will send out a search party." Marley's phone rang. She hurried to her purse on the couch and dug her phone out, placing it to her ear. "Hello? Oh, hey, Mom. Yeah, we're leaving soon. Okay, we'll be careful. I promise. Okay. Mom. Alright. Yes. Yes. I love you, too. Okay, bye. Bye. Bye, Mom."

Benjamin laughed.

Marley returned the phone to her bag and turned to face him. She sighed. "I'm glad she cares. I truly am. But I think she still sees me as an eight-year-old girl."

"It's nice. Enjoy it. Come on, let's get you home. Before you have to answer call number two from your mom." Benjamin walked her to the car. He opened the door for her, letting her slip inside.

As she sank in the seat, so did her heart. Marley hated for her time with Ben to be over. It seemed like each day slipped away faster. She shook her head, wistful.

He took his seat and started the car. Glancing at her, he furrowed his brow. "Everything okay?"

She wouldn't think about leaving. Not yet. She pasted a smile on her face. "Yeah. Everything's fine."

He reached over and squeezed her hand.

"More than fine." She turned her head and looked out the window as he started the car and drove her home. Marley didn't know what she would do in a few weeks when she had to return home. Home to her practice in D.C., where she planned to become a partner. Home to her best friend, whom Marley did miss. Home to the world she'd created where no one knew her as Scarly Marley, but as Marley, the accomplished plastic surgeon. But something nagged at her, tugging at her heart. It whispered from deep within her soul—home was feeling more and more like Blackstone Haven, and Marley didn't know where she belonged anymore.

Chapter 13

December 25, 2019, Wednesday

Benjamin woke Christmas morning with the same excitement he'd felt as a child, even though this Christmas promised no gifts from his parents or family gatherings to attend. But it did promise something incredible—a chance to celebrate at church and spend time with Marley Bakersfield again.

He couldn't stop thinking about their evening baking at his house over the past week. He knew she didn't see herself the way he did—the most gorgeous and kind person he'd ever known. He'd had a crush on her since elementary school, and when she'd walked through the door of his bakery, he couldn't believe it. It seemed like God had given him a second chance—and he wasn't going to blow it. He only wished his mother could spend time with Marley. He knew she'd love her.

He got up, showered, hopped in his car, and headed to church. Walking into the building, he greeted several other attendees and wished them a Merry Christmas. Taking a seat in a pew near the front, he saved Marley and her parents seats. Just in case.

"Benjamin Miller. It's so good to see you. I feel like it's been ages. Have you been hiding from me?"

Ben raised his head, dread filling his gut. "Uh, hi, Stacey. Not hiding from you, but busy. You know, this time of year keeps the bakery hopping."

"Oh, good. Listen, why don't you join my family for dinner tonight? I thought with your mom passing away and not having any close family in town, you would be on your own. I know daddy would love to have you. What do you say?"

Panic coursed through his veins. He could not have any type of dinner with Stacey Blackstone. Especially Christmas dinner. It said commitment. And she definitely was not the woman he wanted to commit himself to in Blackstone Haven.

"Well, Stacey Blackstone, how are you doing?" Marley's mother sidled up to Stacey and gave her and Benjamin a once over.

Stacey turned to Marley's mother and pasted her best artificial smile across her face. "Mrs. Bakersfield, it's so nice to see you. Did your husband join you?"

Marley joined her mother and cast a quick glance at Stacey. Her lips pursed. "He couldn't come with us. His leg bothered him today, and with the crutches, it's hard for him to get in and out of the car. So, he stayed home."

"Oh, well, that's a shame. I love Christmas. My favorite time of year. That's why I told Benjamin I couldn't let him spend it alone, and that he must come over for dinner tonight."

Sweat beaded on the back of Benjamin's neck. "Uh, Stacey—"

"He can't, sorry," Marley spat out the words.

"I can't?" He raised a brow and looked at Marley.

She sent him a pointed look. "No, remember? You already accepted an invitation to have dinner with my family and me. Sorry, Stacey."

Stacey scowled and her eyes flashed with anger. Within seconds, she'd composed herself and replaced her frown with a practiced artificial smile. "I see." She turned her attention to Benjamin again. "In that case, we'll have to plan for another time. Merry Christmas, Benjamin." She started to walk up a few pews to take her seat but spun around. "And let me know if you need help for the bake-off. I happen to know one of the judges—my daddy." She winked.

Marley spoke up, "That won't be necessary. He already has a partner—me."

"Hmm. We'll see. You never know when a medical emergency might arise...or you have to head back to the big city. Anyways,

Benjamin, let me know." She sent him a wave and headed to her seat next to her parents in the front.

Benjamin lifted his eyes to Marley once more. "Sorry about that. She's a determined person."

Marley plopped down in the seat next to him.

Her mother sank next to Marley and leaned across her daughter. "Hah. She's more than determined. Destructive. Distasteful. Damaging. I can't think of any other 'D' words for her right now but give me until the end of the service, and I'm sure I'll come up with some."

Marley snapped her head toward her mother. "Mom! It's Christmas! I don't think you can say those things...especially not today...especially not here."

Mrs. Bakersfield twisted in her seat. "Well, I'm sorry." She leaned across Marley directing her attention to Benjamin, "I'm sorry, Ben. But it's true. And the way that girl tortured Marley during her childhood...really her whole life...well, I can't take any more nonsense from her. There, I've said my piece. I'll behave now."

Marley pressed her lips together, but a small smile tugged at her lips. The church choir gathered on stage, signaling the start of service. She tilted her head closer to Benjamin and whispered, "Sorry."

He gave a soft chuckle. "I'm not. You saved me from an agonizing dinner with Stacey and her family. And your mom's not wrong. How about we ask for forgiveness, focus on God, and enjoy the rest of the day."

"Sounds good to me. And the offer still stands." Marley rose, ready to join in the hymn.

Benjamin stood and whispered once more, "What offer?"

"Christmas dinner with me and my family. Only if you want."

His hand hung at his side. He grinned and inched his fingers closer to hers, clasping her hand in his. "I want."

Marley dipped her head and smiled, starting to sing the first verse of "Joy to the World."

Benjamin didn't know of a more joyful Christmas. If there'd been one, he couldn't recall it. He sang, hope and love filling his heart.

~

Marley looked around the table, scanning the faces. When her eyes settled on Benjamin's, she let them linger. He chatted with her parents, making her mother toss her head back and laugh in a way Marley hadn't seen in years. She didn't listen to the conversation to discover what words had produced such a response from her, but instead studied Benjamin. He was so handsome. His firm jaw, inviting smile, and kind eyes made her heart pound. He'd changed and grown since they were children, but in many ways, he stayed the same, too.

He grinned, lifting his eyes to Marley's as if he knew she'd been watching him.

Marley felt warmth fill her cheeks, and she tucked her head.

Marley's father cleared his throat and folded his hands in front of him on the table. "Let's pray," he directed.

Everyone at the table bowed their head.

"God, thank you for this food, this family, and for, uh, Marley and her efforts at the practice. Amen."

Short and to the point. Typical for her father. The shocking portion came when he'd thanked Marley. Publicly. Her father, a stoic man, held his emotions close and didn't dish out praise often.

Marley opened her eyes and raised her head. She looked at her dad and mouthed, "Thank you."

He gave a barely noticeable nod of the head.

Smiling, Marley opened the white linen napkin folded in the shape of a Christmas tree from her plate. *How did her mother manage to fold it like that?*

Marley's mother rose from her seat and went to the buffet next to the table and brought a large dish to the table. She placed it next to Marley. "Tofu turkey. My own creation. For my Honeybun…I mean, my Marley."

Marley glanced at the golden tofu creation, and her throat tightened. Her mother never acknowledged or remembered Marley's dietary concerns. To some, this might not seem like a big deal. To Marley, this act spoke volumes. Epic proportions. "Mom, wow. Thank you. That was nice of you. It looks great."

Her mom took a seat and waved her hands. "Well, don't let it get cold. Dig in, everyone."

Marley obliged, and the rest of the meal carried through in silence.

Benjamin finished his last bite and wiped his mouth with his napkin. He helped her mother clear the table of its dishes, returned to his seat, and turned his attention to Marley's mother. "Thank you, Mrs. Bakersfield, for the meal. And for inviting me over this evening."

"You are so welcome, Benjamin. I know what a good friend you were to Marley all those years ago when those hooligans gave her a hard time. She has always thought highly of you, and I know you have had a special place in her heart and—"

"Mom!"

Marley's mother shifted her gaze to Marley. She raised her shoulders. "What? It's true, and you're always saying how much you like—"

Marley jumped from her seat. "Okay, then." She fake-yawned. "Benjamin, I'm sure you're tired, and it's getting late. Plus, you told me you've got a lot left to do for the competition. Also, even though it's Christmas week, the sick never sleep, and I have to get an early start on rounding in the morning, and—"

Benjamin chuckled. "It's okay, Marley. I was about to say I needed to head home." He turned to Marley's mother. "Thank you again. I enjoyed spending the evening with your family. I hope you'll come to the Chamber of Commerce Bake-Off Competition on New Year's Eve. Marley and I plan to win."

Marley's mother shifted her eyes to her daughter. "Oh, really? Well, I wouldn't miss it. And you are welcome in our home anytime, Benjamin. Isn't that right, Walter?"

Marley's father had been dozing in his chair as the end-of-dinner conversation transpired. His eyes snapped open, and he uttered, "Hmm, oh, uh, yes, yes, of course. Welcome anytime." He placed his hands on the table, ready to stand. "Sally, will you hand me my crutches. I think I'll go to bed. A good night's sleep is crucial. It's important to get an early start every day. Up before the sun. That's what they taught me in the military, and that's what leads to a productive, efficient life."

Nodding her head, Marley rose, too. "Yes, Dad, we know. Early to bed. Early to rise. I'll walk Benjamin to the door."

Her parents gave Benjamin a final goodbye and headed to their bedroom down the hallway.

Benjamin stood and walked to the front door.

Marley followed him, her stomach twisting and turning with pleasant anxiety. He'd come close to kissing her several times, and she wondered if this might be the moment. The thought both exhilarated and terrified her.

He picked up his heavy wool coat that he'd thrown on the floor by the door and stepped outside onto the porch, turning to face Marley.

She joined him sans jacket and shivered.

"You're freezing. Here, take this." He lifted his coat and draped it across her shoulders. He rubbed her arms with his hands and gave her a squeeze. Gazing down into her eyes, he whispered, "Thank you for tonight. I'm glad I got to spend my Christmas with you."

Tilting her head upward, she breathed, "You're welcome."

He caressed her cheek with his hand. "Marley."

She moved closer. "Yes…"

He dropped his face near hers. "I wanted to tell you…"

She murmured, "Tell me what?"

His lips hovered an inch from hers.

She closed her eyes, ready to open her heart to him. Ready to let her guard down, even a little.

"Marley, you're beautiful and kind, and I—"

Instead of hearing his heartfelt speech or feeling his lips pressed against hers, an upbeat, cheerful rendition of "Deck the Halls" erupted from the neighbor's outdoor Christmas display.

Marley's eyes flew open, and she gasped. "That almost gave me a heart attack." Red and green lights flashed along in sequence to the beat of the music. Normally, she'd consider it festive and inventive, but tonight she found it inopportune and annoying. She frowned.

Benjamin laughed and ran a hand through his hair. "We do not have good timing, do we?"

Laughing, she shook her head. "No, we do not."

Marley's mother's voice called from behind her, "Marley, Honeybun, don't stand out there too long. It's freezing, and you'll catch a cold. I got your father settled. Why don't you come in and have a cup of hot cocoa with me?"

She grinned. "Well, I guess that's my cue. I have a full schedule at work this week, but I'll see you every morning for coffee."

"And New Year's Eve?" He looked down at her.

She nodded. "And New Year's Eve. I'll be there. I don't know why you want me on team Miller with my total rejection of sweets and culinary ineptitude, but I won't miss it. Promise. I better go."

"Yeah…does your mother know hot cocoa has both sugar and dairy in it?"

Marley chuckled as she turned to head inside. "No, probably not. I think she believes if it comes out of a packet, then it doesn't count as real food. I better go get some tea started, or I'm doomed." She walked in and grabbed the door, ready to close it.

"Good night, Marley. See you soon." He sent her a smile and winked.

Marley's legs weakened, and she grabbed the doorframe. "Good night," she whispered before closing the door. She didn't know if they would win the baking competition, but she knew one thing—Benjamin Miller had won her heart, and she didn't want him to let go.

Chapter 14

December 31, 2019, Tuesday

Marley couldn't believe how fast the week had passed.

She'd spent every day bouncing between the clinic and the hospital. She found it astounding how many people made poor decisions with kitchen knives over the holiday season. A turkey or ham appears, and suddenly everyone is the head of their own carving station. *Not.*

Corkie had shadowed Marley several days, and though Marley had questioned taking on the responsibility of mentoring the girl, she'd enjoyed spending time with her. Corkie had a lot of drive and a passion for science, and Marley couldn't help but see a lot of herself in the teen.

Marley wanted to help Corkie. Every day they spent time together, Marley witnessed the girl's confidence grow. Corkie had confided about her troubles at school, and Marley found herself becoming protective of the girl and her feelings. She hoped the "mean girls" left Corkie alone.

As Marley finished her last day of clinic before the big bake-off, she told Corkie goodbye for the day. "Thanks for your help. I appreciate you filing all those paper charts. I can't believe my dad still keeps them. It's creating double work for him, but he's stubborn. Resistant to change."

Sliding the last chart into the filing cabinet, Corkie spun around. "No problem."

"I hope you learned something this week."

Corkie nodded, picking up her coat and backpack from the empty chair where Mrs. Klingensmith usually sat. "I did. Thank you. Oh, grandma told me to tell you she appreciated the time off this past week, and she'll be back and at full force next week. I think she's coming to the bake-off, too."

"Wow, she's the fifth person to tell me today that they are coming."

Corkie shrugged. "It's a big deal around here. I'd say the highlight of the holiday season. I bet the whole town will be there."

Marley's palms began to sweat. "The whole town?" She hoped Stacey and all the kids that still lived here from high school wouldn't bother showing up at the event.

With a big nod, Corkie confirmed Marley's fears, "The. Whole. Town."

"Great. Wonderful. Maybe I—" Marley's phone rang, and she picked it up, glancing at the screen. *Jesse.* She cringed. She's been avoiding her partner's phone calls for the past week. She knew she'd have to tell them something soon about her return, but she'd been walking in a cloud of bliss with Benjamin and didn't want to think about her time coming to an end.

She punched the green button. "Dr. Bakersfield here."

"Dr. Bakersfield, it's Dr. Sloan, Jesse. Checking it to see when you can grace us with your presence again. You're missed around here."

"Uh, thanks, Dr. Sloan. I miss the practice and my patients, too." She took care not to say she missed him. Because she didn't, and he needed no encouragement. "I'm not exactly sure when I'll be back, but I promise it will be soon."

"Any timeframe you could share with us?"

She chewed her fingernail. "Hmm, well, my father is healing well, but he's still on crutches, so I don't think I can get away until he's getting around easier. Maybe a few more weeks?"

Jesse stayed silent.

"Hello?"

"I'm here. I don't think I have to tell you what a crucial time this is in evaluating your position as a partner in the practice."

"No, you do not. I know this is not ideal, but—"

His voice softened, "And I'm sure you know I'd like to see you again soon, too."

"Dr. Sloan, I appreciate you calling to check-in and your concern…and I promise as soon I have a definitive date, I'll let you know. Please let the other partners know I'm trying to handle everything here as quickly as possible."

"Maybe I should drive down there. I could try to help get things wrapped up with your father's practice. Get you back to the real world where you belong?"

Marley immediately stopped chewing her nail and jolted upright. "No, that won't be necessary. You couldn't get privileges here on such short notice. Plus, my father is protective about his practice, and this is a small town, so I'm sure you'd be bored, and," blubbering now, Marley scanned the room for more excuses. Jesse could not come here. She needed more time. More time with Benjamin. More time to find a solution. How could she turn down a prestigious partnership in a top-notch medical practice in D.C.? But how could she leave behind love? She couldn't deny she was falling for Benjamin. He saw her in a way she'd never imagined for herself--he made her feel beautiful.

"I'll let the partners know you'll be back soon, but Marley—"

He hadn't called her by her first name since their non-date date before she left. "Yeah? I mean, yes?"

"Don't make the partners wait too long…or me."

She swallowed hard. "I have to go, Dr. Sloan. I have a volunteer here, and I think she needs something for a patient." Marley made waving gestures toward Corkie.

"Dr. Bakersfield, could you come help me with this?" Corkie shouted.

"Oh, see there, I have to go. Thank you for checking on me. I'll be in touch soon. Bye." Marley turned off her phone, and a sigh escaped from her lips. "Thank you. You saved me."

Corkie scrunched her forehead. "What was that all about?"

"It's a long story, but basically, I'm supposed to be somewhere else right now, someone else right now."

"What do you mean?"

"Hard to explain. Hey, thanks again. You get out of here."

Corkie shrugged, grabbed her stuff, and headed toward the door. She waved, not turning around. "See you at the bake-off, Dr. Bakersfield."

"See you, Corkie." Marley tossed a wave to the girl and walked back to the desk. She plopped into Mrs. Klingensmith's chair and sighed. Tilting her head back, Marley closed her eyes. What would she do? Time was running out. As she considered her options, Marley found no answers. She'd temporarily given up deciding what to do with the rest of her life when her phone rang again. *No more.* She couldn't suffer through another conversation with Dr. Jesse Sloan.

The phone persisted with its ringing, so on the fourth ring Marley picked it up and turned it over to peer at the front. *Tara. Phew.* A smile spread across Marley's face, and her whole body relaxed. Her best friend made everything better. Why hadn't she thought of calling her? Thankfully, Tara had a way of knowing when Marley needed help or advice. She pressed the green button, this time wearing a grin. "Tara, I'm so glad it's you."

"Who else would it be, silly?"

"After the day I've had, it's hard to tell. Anyway, I'm glad it's you."

"How have you been? Any run-ins with the high school horror mob? How's your dad feeling? Most importantly, when do I get you back?" Her best friend rattled off her questions without taking a breath.

"Hi, hello. I missed you, too. I still don't know when I'm coming home. My dad is doing well, but he's still on crutches, so as you can imagine getting around the office and hospital would be a challenge. He has another doctor's appointment after New Year's Eve, so we'll see how that goes."

"And the high-school crew?"

"Ugh. That's another story. I haven't seen too many people around town, but I keep running into Stacey Blackstone."

"Wait, wasn't she the one who gave you that nickname in school? What was it?"

"Don't say it. I can't stand it. And yes, she's the one. The head mean girl, captain of the cheer squad, homecoming queen, and salutatorian. She didn't beat me there. It probably killed her. But I'm trying to rise above and be nice."

Tara snorted. "And how's that going?"

"Hey! I can be nice. It's fine. She keeps showing up when I'm spending time with Benjamin. I'm one hundred percent sure she has her eyes on him, but I can't do anything about that."

"And how's Benjamin?"

"He's good, great actually. He's handsome, sweet, and thoughtful. But I'm supposed to come home soon. Remember? You were trying to get me to return minutes ago."

"Yeah, I know. It's true. I do miss you like crazy, but I want you to be happy. You sound happy. Maybe staying in Blackstone Haven wouldn't be the worst thing in the world."

Marley shook her head. "I don't know, Tara. I'm supposed to come home. I'm supposed to make partner. That's the plan." Tears filled Marley's eyes, and she sobbed softly.

"Hmm. I'm thinking I need to come there. It sounds like you need a friend."

"Tara, you don't have to do that."

"I'm on call the next few days, but I'll try to get someone to cover for me and get there as soon as possible. When I know what day I can leave, I'll text you. Okay?"

Marley sniffled. "Okay. If you're sure. But really, Tara, you don't have to do it."

"I know. But you're my best friend. You'd do it for me. So, what else is on your agenda for the day?"

"I need to go home to change clothes, and then I'm supposed to head over to the bake-off."

"I still can't believe you're assisting in a baking competition. You know there will be sugar and dairy in the things you make, right?"

"Ha-ha. I know. It's for a good cause. And it means a lot to Benjamin."

"Oh, it's for Benjamin, huh." Tara made kissing sounds into the phone.

"You're a four-year-old. You know that?"

Tara giggled. "I'll talk to you soon. Tell Benjamin I said hello, and I'm excited to attend the wedding."

"The wedding?"

"Between you and him. Marley and Benjamin sitting in a tree, K—"

"I'm hanging up now," Marley shouted into the phone, "a four-year-old. Love you, bye." She turned the phone off and shoved it in her purse. Relief rushed through her that she hadn't let Tara finish the schoolyard chant. Her face burned, and she didn't need any reminders about kissing or marrying Benjamin Miller. She had enough of those thoughts swirling around her mind without any help.

~

Benjamin knotted his black satin tie and smoothed it. It looked silly. *What baker wore a suit?* Of course, he'd take the jacket off and replace it with his white apron during the bake-off. The town made the competition a spectacle, and he knew everyone would dress up for it. He didn't have a choice, but the promise of seeing Marley brought a smile to his face.

As he shrugged into his suit jacket, he went through a mental checklist. Had he forgotten anything? He'd packed the ingredients, bowls, spoons, measuring cups, and a change of clothes in case of a mishap. He couldn't think of anything else he needed. Marley told him she'd meet him by 4 p.m. at his bakery before heading to Blackstone High School, where the competition would take place.

This list of entries posted to the front of the school door showed ten competitors. They each had been assigned a different time slot to use one of the kitchen ovens, so timing the preparation and bake of the cinnamon rolls would be challenging. He'd told Marley she could dress casually and change after they made their creations. Still, he didn't want to bother with worrying about his clothes during the competition. Hence the suit now.

The rules of the competition stated they had to prepare enough samples for voting. Everyone who attended the bake-off--guests, competitors, and judges--got a vote to narrow the entries down. Once the selection of the final three occurred, the judges made their choice of the winner.

"Hello?" Marley's voice echoed through the front of the bake shop.

"I'm in the back. Hang on, I'll be out in a second," he called.

"Take your time," she trilled.

He scanned the back of the kitchen to ensure he hadn't left anything crucial behind before heading out front. As he came through the doorway between the two rooms, his eyes fell upon Marley, and he stopped. "Wow. You look amazing." She didn't have her dress clothes on yet, but she looked stunning. She wore dark jeans, a plain white shirt underneath a gray coat, and boots. Her hair hung in loose waves down her back, and her eyes lit up with her smile.

She gave him an approving look. "Hey, you look great--very spiffy."

He glanced down at his attire and gave a small shrug. "Thanks. Not my first choice for a bake-off, but I don't want to chance running low on time during the competition."

Furrowing her brow, she lifted her thumb to her lips and chewed on her nail. "Should I change now? I didn't want to get flour all over my satin gown, but maybe I should risk it. Will I look ridiculous if I go like this?"

He shook his head. "No, you're fine. I'll make sure you have time to change. As long as one of us stays with the rolls, we should be good."

She quit fiddling with her nail. "Okay. Is your car loaded already, or do you need me to carry something?"

He surveyed the bakery, letting his eyes hover over the counter, display case, and the back bar. He didn't see anything he'd missed. "No, I think I got it all…including the most important thing--our secret ingredient." He grinned.

She raised a brow. "The Marley and Benjamin twist?"

His grin widened. "Exactly." One final glance eased his worries he'd forgotten something, and he walked out from behind the counter. He stepped toward Marley and offered his hand. "Ready?"

She took his hand and smiled. "Ready. Let's go."

He led her out of the bakery to his packed-to-the-brim car and helped her inside. Once he took his seat, he whispered a prayer to God for favor. Although the competition was for charity providing funds to the children's floor of the hospital, it also carried bragging rights. And this year, a private donor had upped the stakes—the winner would receive $25,000, and the benefactor promised to match the contribution to the hospital as well.

He'd wondered if the mystery contributor might be one of the judges. Benjamin had tried to find out who the judges were for the competition this year with no success. For once, the Blackstone Haven rumor mill failed him.

Marley reached for his hand again and gave it a squeeze. "Nervous?"

He swallowed. "Yeah, a little. If I don't win the prize money...I don't think the bakery will make it. The idea of losing it, after all my mother did to build it...well, I'd hate to sell it, but sometimes I wonder if it would be the best option."

She squeezed his hand again. "Hey, look at me."

He met her gaze, and his heart pounded.

"You are not going to lose the bakery. It's too important to you. I know how much it meant to your mom and how much it means to you. We will make the best cinnamon rolls this town has ever tasted, and we're going to win the bake-off and the prize money. You're going to keep your bakery, and nothing is going to stop us. Okay?"

He grinned. "Okay." Putting the car into drive, he pulled away from the bakery, leaving his doubts and concerns behind. Or most of them. He still didn't want to think about how time continued to slip away for him and Marley. Sometimes he wondered if he should sell the bakery, the farm, and close up shop to his business and his heart. But then he'd think about her smile, her eyes, and all the goodness that made up Marley Bakersfield, and he knew. He knew he had to stay and fight. He had to fight for what his heart wanted-- to save his mother's business and the love between him and the beautiful doctor.

Chapter 15

December 31, 2019, Tuesday

As Benjamin's car pulled into the paved parking lot of the high school, Marley's heart beat faster. This time, she couldn't blame it on Benjamin. As he put the car in park, Marley placed her hand on the door handle, ready to open it. Her eyes lifted and she saw Stacey Blackstone glide across the parking lot carrying a cardboard box with two girls Marley recognized from high school in tow. Marley froze.

Benjamin had been ready to open his door but paused, noticing her hesitation. "You okay?"

She stared ahead, her eyes following the trio as they sauntered and cackled all the way to the front door. "No."

Benjamin's followed her eye line. "Oh. I'm sorry, I didn't know she'd be here today. Although she's at every town event, so I shouldn't be surprised. But hey," he murmured, placing a hand on her shoulder, "ignore them."

Softening at his touch, Marley turned her head towards him. "I'll try."

"Come on, I'll be there with you the entire time. Promise." He caressed her shoulder.

She gave a tiny nod and summoned a half-hearted smile to her face.

He hopped out of the car and came around to open her door.

She stepped out and waited as he unloaded the pile of boxes they would need for the competition.

"Woah, that's a lot of stuff."

He bent over and picked up a smaller plastic tub and handed it to her.

She had her purse and a garment bag she'd retrieved from the backseat in her hand. Shifting those items to one arm, she accepted the tub from him. "You can give me more to carry. I won't break."

He leaned over again and lifted a stack of three larger tubs, groaning. Carrying them as they teetered, he muffled from behind the plastic tower, "I've got it. Follow me."

She wondered if she shouldn't lead the way since her vision remained unobstructed but didn't want to interrupt his balancing act. Walking into the same building where she'd attended her high school prom, Marley's hands trembled. She clasped them around her load tighter, trying to steady them and her nerves.

Take deep breaths. It's not the same as back then. But then why did it feel the same? Marley couldn't help but think she wasn't good enough. Not good enough then, and not good enough now. She felt scarred, broken, and damaged.

Benjamin stopped at the door, waiting for her to open it as he couldn't see beyond the mountain of supplies he lugged.

She walked around him and reached for the door. "Sorry, let me get that. I zoned out for a minute."

He slipped through the entrance and sat the stack down on the floor. "Thanks. Let's go to the kitchen and find out where we set up our station. I can come back and get these once we know where we are assigned."

"Sounds good." Marley walked behind him, recalling with each step difficult memories from the last time she'd walked this hallway. It had been her first and last high school prom night. She'd worn a silk, red floor-length gown and spent an hour in a salon chair having her hair crafted into a chignon, careful to conceal her scar. For the first time in her entire life, she'd felt almost pretty. Her mind drifted back to a painful memory from that night. She'd bumped into Stacey as soon as she'd arrived at the prom.

"Well, well, if isn't Scarly Marley all dressed up," the cackling voice had called from down the same hallway.

"Stacey, leave me alone." Marley had continued her processional, keeping her head down, trying to escape the mean girl.

"What? I'm not doing anything. I only commented on how nice you looked. You know, it would be a shame if something happened to such a lovely gown."

As Marley took her first step through the entrance to the dance, an obstruction caught her underfoot, causing her to topple forward and fall. She hit a girl holding a cup of punch before thudding against the floor face first.

"Awe, poor Scarly Marley. You need to watch where you're going."

Marley pushed her upper body up and looked down. Her dress she'd painstakingly selected with her mother was now drenched with punch. Heat filled her face, and she tucked her head in further as she stood.

Several of Stacey's cohorts gathered and joined in the teasing, pointing, and giggling.

Spinning on her heel, Marley ran from the dance, down the hallway, all the way home. She couldn't prove it, but Marley had always suspected Stacey had tripped her. That night she'd pledged to herself to leave town and never return after graduation. Walking down the same hallway that led to this resolution brought back the feelings of embarrassment, resentment, and rejection.

Marley didn't realize she'd stopped walking until Benjamin called to her, "Marley, something wrong?"

She stood rooted but responded, "Sorry…thinking about the last time I came here for a party."

His face sagged. "I forgot about that…I should've thought… I'm sorry. Are you going to be okay to do this?"

Of course, he knew about prom. Everyone in the town had talked about it for at least a week. Marley couldn't let those girls defeat her; this town defeat her. She gave a firm nod. "No, I'm fine. Let's win this thing."

He gave a slow smile. "Well, okay, then. Let's win this thing." He turned around and continued down the hallway to find their station.

Once checking in with the competition coordinator, Benjamin started unpacking boxes.

Marley unloaded items one at a time, trying to get organized.

After everything appeared ready, Benjamin put a white apron over his dress pants and shirt. He handed an identical one to Marley.

She took it and draped it over her head atop her jeans and shirt. Marley thought about changing into her gown now so she wouldn't be rushed later to present their concoctions. However, considering her history with designer gowns and this school, she thought better of it.

He stepped closer behind her and grabbed the thin ties on the apron's sides.

She became acutely aware of his proximity and could feel his breath on the back of her neck. Goosebumps rose on her arms, and she had to remind herself to breathe.

He pulled the strings tighter and tied the apron in a knot, letting his hand linger on her low back.

Turning around, Marley raised her head, meeting his eyes. She felt herself inching closer to him.

A voice from a speaker on the stage interrupted the moment, "Hello." The gentleman tapped on the microphone.

Marley turned to see who stood on stage addressing the crowd of competitors. She gulped. *Stacey's father, Mr. Blackstone.* "Hello, everyone. Good evening. First, I want to thank all of you for donating your talents and time to this wonderful cause. If tonight goes as well as years past, I think we can assure a great financial boost to the children's wing of the hospital. As many of you know, an anonymous donor offered an additional cash prize to the winner and a matching contribution to the hospital. It's a win-win for everyone."

The crowd erupted in cheers and applause, and Stacey's father grinned and waved, obviously enjoying the attention. "Now, let me officially start the competition. On your mark, get set...bake,' he shouted into the microphone before leaving the stage.

All the bakers at surrounding tables scurried and jumped into motion.

"I guess we'd better get started." Marley straightened out her apron and stood ready for her orders.

Benjamin swallowed before answering, "Right. Okay, you take this and start adding all the dry ingredients to the bowl." He handed her an index card with a list of items and a large silver mixing bowl.

"I'm going to get all the wet things together. We have at least two hours until our scheduled oven time, but I want to make sure we're ready when it's our turn."

She nodded and took the things from him and hopped into action.

The two of them worked in silence for a while, focusing on their own tasks, careful to not make a mistake.

Marley had checked off each item with a pen as she measured and added it, and when she got to salt on the list, she paused. *Where was the salt?* She rifled through the small bottles and containers in the plastic tub. *Sugar, cinnamon, ground cloves, baking soda, baking powder…no salt.* "Uh, Benjamin?"

He whisked an egg with fury and lifted his eyes to meet hers. Sweat beaded across his brow.

Hmm. He looked stressed.

"Yeah, Marley, something wrong?" His brow furrowed deeper.

"Uh, no. It's nothing. I think I might have left something in the car… I'll be right back."

He nodded toward his suit jacket on top of one of the tubs. "Okay, the keys are in my jacket pocket."

She smiled and reached for them. "Thanks."

He already had returned to his whisking and didn't seem to hear her.

She hurried to the car and scrounged around it, hoping the salt had fallen out in the backseat. After a thorough search of the vehicle, she came to the awful realization it had not. *Now what? Maybe there's salt in the cafeteria kitchen?* Buoyed by the idea, she ran inside and snaked her way around people to the high school's kitchen. The cafeteria served as a gymnasium and auditorium. It was where all the competitors worked at separate tables functioning as baking stations.

Slipping into the kitchen's busy hub where other competitors took turns at the ovens and stovetops, Marley understood why Benjamin had brought his own hotplate and extension cord. The kitchen looked like a tornado had blown through it.

She tried to weave her way past others unnoticed until she found a pantry near the back. Marley opened the door to it and saw it overflowed with everyday cooking and baking items. The big blue container with the words "salt" written across it shone like a beacon of hope. She retrieved it and hurried back to Benjamin.

"Hey, I thought I'd lost my partner." He continued stirring but gave her a half-grin.

"Nope, I had to get something." She held up the salt container.

He didn't look at her but kept his head down, focused on the mixture he'd been stirring. "Great. Okay, I think we're ready to add it all together and get the dough rising."

Marley mixed in the salt and handed her ingredients to Benjamin.

Two hours later, their dough looked better than the last time they'd practiced. They'd placed in the apples and their secret ingredient, Benjamin's black walnuts, and panned the dough, then let it sit.

A volunteer stopped by their station. She had a pen placed behind her ear and held a clipboard. Glancing at her list, she raised her eyes and peered at them over wire-rimmed glasses. "Benjamin Miller?"

"Yes, that's' me."

"I believe it is your turn in the kitchen. You'll have one hour with the oven."

"Thank you, ma'am."

She tipped her head and carried on down the aisle, moving to the next station.

Benjamin gathered two large metal pans and nodded for Marley to do the same.

She followed behind, careful not to trip and spill their hard work all over the floor.

Once inside the kitchen, they alternated putting as many pans as would fit into the oven, carrying on with nervous chatter between each grouping as they waited for the batch to bake.

One hour and many frazzled nerves later, Benjamin finished applying the cream cheese icing glaze to the final batch. "There, done."

"They look amazing." Marley placed a hand on the top of Benjamin's back. "Your mom would be proud."

He gazed down at her, his eyes glistening. "Thanks. And thank you for all your help. I couldn't have done it without you."

"You're welcome, but I'm sure you could have managed." Marley peered at the large clock on the cafeteria wall and gasped. "I better go change. The doors open to the public soon, and the judging begins in twenty minutes."

"You go get dressed, and I'll clean up here and put on my jacket." He wiped his hands on a towel.

Marley grabbed her garment bag and hurried off to find a bathroom. She changed into her emerald mermaid-cut gown and black heels. Brushing her hair out, she smoothed her bangs to the side, covering her scar better, and pinned them in place with a decorative clip. Her hair shone like a fiery wave, glimmering in the light.

Pulling a compact and tube of lipstick out of her purse, Marley touched up her makeup-- wiping away the sweat from her efforts with cream-colored powder and slicking on a bright red lip color that matched her hair.

Staring at herself in the mirror, her pulse quickened, thinking about her evening with Benjamin, the competition, and the future. Her jade eyes looked happier than they had in years. She saw love in them—love for Benjamin, but also, perhaps, love for herself.

Marley straightened her posture and put the makeup back in her bag. Exiting the bathroom, she nearly plowed over someone.

"Watch where you're going," the caustic voice spat.

"Stacey, sorry, I didn't see you there."

"My, my, don't you look fancy."

Marley glanced at her dress, unsure of how to take the compliment. "Uh, thanks, Stacey. I better go. The judging is about to start."

"Yes, hurry, but watch your step... you'd hate to trip and fall again like last time."

Marley's chest pounded, and her throat ached. *Don't let her get a rise. Stay calm.* "I'll be careful, Stacey. Thanks for your concern." Before her nemesis could respond, Marley took off toward Benjamin and what she hoped would be a new beginning. Maybe she had put away Scarly Marley once and for all.

~

Gratitude rushed through Benjamin as Marely stepped from the hallway into the cafeteria again. *She looked stunning.* He always found her beautiful, but tonight her radiance shone like a beacon from within. Taking in her wavy hair and figure in the green gown which accentuated her curves, his jaw dropped.

She joined him at their station and arched a brow. "What?"

"It's…you look…wow. You look incredible," Benjamin stammered.

She tossed her head back and laughed. "Thanks. You do, too. Look great, I mean."

He started to open his mouth to share his appreciation for her help and tell her more about how much she meant to him. At that moment, however, one of the judges circulating the room stopped in front of them.

Benjamin jumped into business owner mode and explained his recipe and the significance behind it.

The first of three judges took a bite and broke into a wide grin. She murmured something about it tasting like heaven and moved on to the next table after making a few notes on her clipboard.

The same process followed for the next judge.

In the competition, the final decision maker, Stacey's father, stopped before them and rubbed his hands together. "Well, Dr. Bakersfield, it's so nice to see you pitching in and helping the community. Even if it is only for a little while before you head back to the big city."

Marley stiffened. She placed a smile on her face, but it looked forced. "Happy to help. I think you'll find Benjamin's cinnamon rolls to be the best entry in the competition."

He gave a slight nod. "We'll see." He picked up a paper plate holding a cinnamon roll on it, lifting the gooey creation to his lips. He took a bite and appeared to attempt to hide his pleasure. He sat the plate down again and wiped his hands on a napkin before picking up his clipboard again and writing something down. "Good," he uttered before moving to the next contestant.

Marley sighed. "Well, I've blown it for you."

Benjamin shook his head and continued to hand out samples to attendees of the event. "Would you stop it? He's a tough guy. It has nothing to do with you."

She rolled her eyes. "Oh, it has everything to do with me. I told you he wants to buy my dad's medical practice…or well, the hospital does at least, so it might as well be him. And his daughter loathes me. And there's something weird between him and my dad that I still haven't unearthed, but I know I'm not imagining it."

He stopped passing around dishes and turned to Marley, taking both her hands in his. "Listen, you have been incredible. Win or lose, I couldn't have done this without you. If he doesn't pick me, or if the other judges don't pick me, it's not your fault."

"Yeah, but if you don't win, what will happen to your mother's bakery? To the farmhouse?" To us, she wanted to say but didn't.

"Let's not think about it. We still might win."

A woman's voice called from the stage, "May I have everyone's attention?" She waited until the chatter died down before speaking again, "Thank you all for your time and effort today. You've all worked hard and done a wonderful job."

Everyone in the room gave a polite clap then quieted again.

"I think I speak for the entire Chamber of Commerce when I say the decision about the winner for the bake-off today proved a challenge. Everyone's entries were delightful. However, we do have to select one winner. The winning entry today surprised us with creativity, flavor, and heart. May I call to the stage the winner of the 2019 Chamber of Commerce Bake-Off Competition…. drum roll, please…."

An artificial drumroll sounded across the speakers as the woman paused.

"Benjamin Miller and his delicious apple-cinnamon nut rolls!"

The crowd erupted in applause and cheering, and Benjamin's mouth fell open.

Marley jumped up and down and embraced him in a hug. "You won! You won!" She released him from the exuberant embrace.

He stood still.

She gave him a gentle shove. "Go on, go up there, and get your prize."

Benjamin took one small step before turning to her. Grinning, he picked up Marley and spun her around before placing her down and heading to the front. Taking the stairs to the stage at a slight jog, Benjamin strode across the stage with exuberance.

As he approached the microphone, the woman handed him a trophy, certificate, and a large check. He accepted them, and she moved aside for him to say a few words. "Um, hello. Hi, uh, I have to say this is…unexpected. Thank you for selecting my cinnamon rolls as the best entry today. I know my mother would be proud because she loved this town and loved baking for it. I have to say thanks to my partner today, Dr. Marley Bakersfield." He tipped the trophy in Marley's direction.

She blushed and gave a small wave.

Staring into her eyes, he spoke to Marley, "I couldn't have done it without her. And I think I speak for the rest of the town when I say it is an honor to have you with us, and we hope you'll grace us with your presence for a lot longer." He shifted his eyes back to the crowd. "Thank you again. Happy New Year everyone."

The crowd clapped and whistled, and several people near Marley patted her back and gave their congratulations.

Benjamin took the stairs off the stage and made his way back to Marley. Sliding next to her, he dipped his head close to her ear. "Thank you. For everything."

She smiled, and her cheeks flushed a deeper pink. Looking at him through her eyelashes, she asked, "So, what's next?"

He didn't know if Marley was referring to their relationship or the rest of the evening. Still, the answer came to them in the form of the announcer on stage.

"Attention, everyone. If I may make one more announcement. With the conclusion of this year's Bake-Off, I want to encourage you to enjoy the second portion of our little celebration. The tables will be moved away, and a local band has donated their time to play for us. Feel free to sample the remaining baked goods and grab someone's hand and drag them to the dance floor. Let's ring in the New Year the Blackstone Haven way!"

More cheers erupted from the crowd, and people started packing away tools, utensils and handing out the remaining food. Volunteer staff hoisted tables and chairs and shifted them to the periphery of the room. With an open dance floor created, couples paired up as the band took to the wooden stage.

Benjamin offered his hand to Marley, guiding her to the center of the room. He couldn't take his eyes off her—she looked stunning in her green dress and heels. Placing a hand on her low back,

Benjamin spun Marley around the floor, offbeat to the music, but enjoying himself, nonetheless.

Tossing her head back and laughing, Marley lit up the room.

The minutes turned to hours, and before Benjamin realized it, the band announced they were taking a break to let the crowd grab a glass of cider for the midnight toast. He stopped swaying and looked down at Marley, still holding her hand. "Hey, why don't we get a glass and take it outside? Get some fresh air?"

She gazed up at him, breathless from the spinning. "Sounds good to me." She followed him to the drink table and then out the gymnasium door. The stars overhead twinkled in the sky, casting a golden glow to the snow-covered ground below. "Wow, it's beautiful tonight."

Taking a step closer to Marley, he stared into her eyes. "It certainly is." He started to speak but didn't know where to start.

The door remained cracked to the dance, and he could hear the announcer beginning the countdown to midnight. "10, 9, 8, 7…"

He grazed his thumb across Marley's cheek and cupped her jaw with his fingers. Tilting her chin upward, he brought her lips closer to his.

"6, 5, 4, 3…"

Marley closed her eyes and leaned closer, her hand sliding around the back of Benjamin's neck and weaving her fingers into his hair.

"2, 1…Happy New Year!"

Benjamin pressed his mouth against Marley's soft, red lips, and he felt her melt into him. The kiss lasted for seconds, but to him, it seemed like an eternity, and he didn't want it to end. As the notes of "Auld Lang Syne" carried outside, he grudgingly pulled away.

Looking into Benjamin's eyes, Marley sent him a slow smile. Her cheeks and nose flushed, either from the cold air or the passion of the kiss or maybe both.

"Marley, I…I love you. I think I've loved you forever. Since we were kids."

"I love you, too, Benjamin. You've always made me feel safe…and cared for…and beautiful."

"That's because you are cared for, and you are beautiful…on the outside and the inside. You're the most beautiful person I know.

I realize you're supposed to leave soon…to go back to your practice, but I—"

She placed her fingers on his lips, stopping the conversation. "Let's not think about it tonight. This evening has been perfect, and I'm not leaving right now. Let's focus on us tonight. And how wonderful everything is at this exact moment."

His throat tightened. He wanted to beg her to stay. To tell her he wanted and needed her in his life. That he could save his mother's bakery and make it his own, now. He could keep the farm and create a wonderful life for the two of them. If she would only stay. Instead, he nodded and murmured, "Okay," and dipped his head toward hers again. He touched his lips to Marley's once more before leading her out of the crisp night air.

Tonight, had been perfect. Benjamin had gotten everything he'd ever wanted—his mother's bakery saved, a chance to make the business better, and a shot at love. As long as Marley Bakersfield didn't break his heart into a million pieces.

Chapter 16

January 7, 2020, Tuesday

Marley hummed as she drove to work each morning the following week. Although it had been a few days since she'd seen Benjamin beyond swinging by the bakery for coffee, she still recalled the feeling of his lips upon hers.

She pressed her fingers to her lips and smiled.

She'd made her own coffee at home this morning, but as she drove down Main Street, Marley decided to stop and grab another cup. Plus, she couldn't pass up an excuse to see Benjamin.

Parking her car, she lifted her eyes and noted the shiny, black SUV with dark rims and extra chrome on the bumper in the space in front of her. It looked familiar. The driver had already left, and it sat empty.

Gasping, Marley's hand flew to her mouth. *Jesse Sloan. The car belonged to Jesse Sloan. Oh no! What was he doing here? Well, that was a ridiculous question.* She knew the answer. He came to convince her to return to the practice; to her job. He'd left one voice message, a text message, and an email she'd ignored for the past two days. She didn't want to face the truth—she had a decision to make. Should she stay, or should she go?

Grabbing her purse, Marley clamored out of the car like a spendthrift going to a 90% off sale. *Where could he have gone?* Her eyes scanned the sidewalks, darting from one storefront to the next. When they settled on the sign to Benjamin's bakery, her heart sank. *Of course.* Somehow, someway he'd made it to the one place she didn't want her old life and new life to collide.

Glancing both ways crossing the street, Marley shoved open the door to the bakery and burst inside, out of breath. "Benjamin, I have to tell you something—" *Too late.*

Benjamin stood behind the counter, wearing an irritated look on his face. Jesse leaned against the counter on the opposite side. When Benjamin met Marley's eyes, they held hurt and confusion.

Jesse turned around at the commotion of Marley's entrance, and a confident grin erupted. "Marley. You look amazing. I talked with Mr. Miller here and told him how much you've been missed at the hospital in D.C., especially at the practice. I told him I came here to convince you to come home. The rest of the partners are meeting later this week to make a final decision about your partnership, and I know how important that is to you. I didn't want to leave anything to chance. Plus, I'm sure your father can find someone to fill in for him until he's fully on his feet again."

Marley clenched her fists at her side. *How dare he come here like this and pretend to know what she wanted. But what did she want? Hadn't partnership been the plan all along? Life in D.C.? Far away from her hometown and all the pain it had caused in the past?* That's what she'd thought before she returned to Blackstone Haven. Now, she didn't know. Now, she felt her heart nudging her to stay. She'd found a sense of purpose in caring for the kind townspeople, and her heart had opened to Benjamin. Was she ready to close it up and pack it away again? "Dr. Sloan, you didn't have to make the trip. I planned to call you back to discuss all of this later in the week."

Benjamin tightened his jaw and busied himself with shoving a few muffins in a white bag, crumpling the top of it with force.

Jesse continued, "Well, I didn't think the practice, or I could stand to have you away much longer." He turned to Benjamin. "She must have told you we have a special relationship. Before she left town, we had a romantic dinner to discuss the future. Isn't that right, Marley?" He looked back at her and raised a brow.

Marley stepped forward, ready to explain her dinner with Benjamin, but didn't get the chance.

Benjamin shoved the white bag of muffins toward Jesse and spat out the words, "I've got to take care of some things in the back.

Enjoy your muffins. I'm sure you'll both be happy together." He stormed off to the storage room in the back of the bakery before Marley could speak.

She stood rooted, her mouth hanging open and tears filling her eyes.

Jesse spun around and sauntered up to her, carrying the bag with him. "If that's the small-town hospitality you were telling me about, then I'm not impressed. Ready to go?"

Marley couldn't believe Benjamin had left like that. He hadn't let her say anything. *How could he think she'd discard him after all they'd been through together? Maybe he didn't feel as strongly for her as she'd thought. Perhaps, she didn't belong here after all.* She gave a small nod of her head, avoiding Jesse's gaze. "Let's go. I have to swing by the practice, but you're welcome to follow me. We can talk there."

He opened the door for her and let her step through before following behind.

She peered over her shoulder before crossing the street, casting one final glance at Benjamin's bakery. *How could everything crumble so quickly?*

~

As the door closed, indicating his customers had left, Benjamin stepped out from his hiding place in the storage room. He should have fought for her. He shouldn't have let her go with that overconfident city slicker, but the guy had caught him off guard. Benjamin had felt so sure about their relationship, especially after New Year's Eve. How could he have gotten it so wrong? He hadn't...she had to be confused. *Yes, that had to be it.* He nodded his head and decided as soon as the bakery closed, he'd head to her parent's house and make his case, declaring his love for her again. He had to try. She was worth it.

Benjamin tore off his apron and hung it on the hook on the wall behind the counter. He grabbed his keys and flipped the lights off on his way out the door, locking it behind him. Hopping in the car, he said a silent prayer. *God, please work out things with Marley.*

He headed toward her medical practice, rehearsing in his mind the words he wanted to say. He hoped she'd listen. He prayed she'd stay.

~

Marley walked into the medical practice and had never been so glad to see her father in her entire life. "Dad, what are you doing here?"

He stood and wobbled, trying to steady himself on his crutches. "I wanted to stop by and check on things. See how you're doing and get updated on our patients. Who's your guest?" He nodded toward Jesse, who'd followed her into the office.

Shoot. "Oh, Dad, uh, this is Jesse, I mean, Dr. Sloan. He works with me back in D.C. He stopped by to check on me and discuss some cases from my old practice. I think he was about to leave, though, and go find something to eat besides muffins. Isn't that right, Dr. Sloan?" She stared at him, willing him to take the hint. "That way, I can discuss some matters with my father, and then we can talk about the D.C. practice afterward? Would that work, Dr. Sloan?"

He opened his mouth and looked like he might object, but her eyes must have contained an intensity he didn't dare challenge because he closed his mouth and gave a short nod. "Sure. I'll see if there's a deli or something in town that serves something more healthful than that bakery. Maybe a salad or spinach smoothie. I'll be back in an hour."

"Oh, wait." She didn't want him returning here and chancing another run-in between him and her father. "Why don't you meet me at the hospital in an hour? I need to do evening rounds on a few patients. Okay?"

He headed to the door and opened it, pausing. "Dr. Bakersfield, I'll see you in one hour. We have a lot to discuss."

Marley turned away from Jesse and focused on her father.

Her father tilted his head toward his office. "Why don't you sit down. You look like you could use a rest." He headed that direction as fast as the crutches allowed.

Marley hoisted her purse higher on her shoulder but obliged.

Taking his seat behind the massive desk, he pointed to a chair across from him with one of his crutches' tips. "Have a seat."

Plopping into the chair, Marley heaved a sigh.

"Tough day?" He raised his forehead.

She gave him a wry grin. "You could say that, Dad."

He lifted his eyes to the medal on the wall.

She let her eyes follow his. He'd never shared about what he'd done to earn it or anything else about his time in the military.

"Did I ever tell you how I got that?" He pointed to the medal.

She glanced at the medal hanging inside a glass shadow box. Shaking her head, she said, "No."

"I received that from serving on my tour overseas in 1980. Serving as a medic proved an incredible honor and responsibility. Unfortunately, not everyone shared my views. Someone from this town joined my unit. His lack of respect and obedience led to a considerable error and put several lives at risk—some of whom I had to work hard to save. Her father sent her a leveled stare. "Do you have any idea who that might have been?"

Marley swallowed hard. "Stacey's father?"

Giving a small nod, her father confirmed her speculation. "Exactly. Of course, he's a smooth talker and did a good job covering his mistakes, but I knew about what he'd done. He left the post he'd been assigned. Instead, he went off with a group of locals, including some young ladies, and his absence led to a breach in security. He should have been dishonorably discharged, but he wasn't. Blackstone knows that I know what he did, and about his true character."

Marley sighed. "So, that's why he doesn't like our family. And why he wants to take away your practice."

Her dad nodded again. "That and upon our return, we both met and fell in love with the same woman...but she chose me."

Now Marley's jaw nearly hit the floor. "Mom? Mom was part of a love triangle? My mom? The sweet homemaker who bakes daily. No way."

Her dad cleared his throat and gave a gruff, "Way."

"Wow."

"So, after all of that, he carries a lot of resentment. It seems. Do you know why I don't want to give up the medical practice?"

"Because you can't stand Mr. Blackstone?"

He gave her a half-grin. "I admit, he's not my favorite person, but I try to follow God's word and forgive him for what he's done. But that's not why I don't want to sell."

She peered at the medal on the wall once more before settling her eyes on her dad. "Then, why? Why not sell it and take a break? Take mom on vacation?"

"Because I started this practice from the ground up for you and your mother. For my family. And for this community. I can't abandon it, and my patients, especially since Stacey's father only wants it because he knows how much it means to me. When your mother chose me over him, he couldn't stand it. It's been like this ever since then. So now he wants to take away the only thing he can---my practice. Because of what it represents--my family, my service, and my heart. He wants to rip it away."

"I'm sorry, Dad. I didn't know about any of this."

"Don't you see I can't let him do it? Not to mention, I think you'd be happy here. You seem to have found someone special, and I think the town is growing on you. It's not the same place you left all those years ago. And you're not the same person. You're stronger, more confident."

"Dad, I don't see how I can stay. I have my own practice in D.C., my own patients. What would I tell them? What would I do? Besides, I can't imagine there's a significant need for a plastic surgeon in Blackstone Haven. Can you?"

Her father tapped the tips of his fingers together. "Then you do a mix of general procedures and plastics. You're double-boarded. It's possible." He raised his brow.

"Dad, I---" Marley's pager beeped. She pushed on the button and peered down at it. "It's the hospital. I have to call them back."

Her father dipped his head and brought his steepled fingers to his lips.

Marley dug her phone out of her purse and punched in the numbers to the hospital. "Hello, yes, this is Dr. Bakersfield. What's going on?" She paused, listening to the person on the other end of the line. "What kind of accident? Of course, of course. Okay, yes, I'm coming. I'll be there in ten minutes."

Her father raised his eyebrows. "What was that?"

Marley shoved her phone in her purse and grabbed her keys, standing. "It's Corkie. I have to go, Dad. I'm sorry. She's been in a car accident and suffered a lot of facial trauma. I can't leave her in the hands of someone else. I need to know she's taken care of myself."

He grabbed her hand, stopping her for a moment. "I understand, but Marley?"

"Yeah, Dad?"

"Consider my proposal. It could be good for you." He squeezed her hand before releasing it.

She shook her head. "I can't talk about it right now. I've got to go. Will you be okay here on your own? Should I call mom?"

He shook his head. "No, I'll be fine. I've got these." He lifted his crutches beside his chair.

"Promise me you won't overdo it. Sit there and drink your coffee," she nodded toward his half-full cup of coffee on the corner of his desk, "and take it easy until Mom comes to pick you up. I wish I hadn't given Mrs. Klingensmith the day off."

He waved her away with both hands. "I'll be fine. But we aren't done discussing the practice." He nodded toward the door. "Go take care of that girl."

She cast a final glance at her father, noting how small he looked sitting behind his desk with the crutches at his side. She felt terrible leaving him like this, but she couldn't let Corkie down. Darting out the door of her father's office, she ran for the front door, shoved it open, and gulped in a breath of air as she made a beeline for her car. She jumped in and started it, speeding out of the parking lot and kicking gravel up as she left.

Marley didn't know what she'd do about her life; her father's practice, her own practice, the townspeople who'd come to rely on her, or the mess she'd made of her relationship with Benjamin. Shaking her head, she focused on the road. She couldn't think about any of it right now. Now, all she could focus on was helping Corkie.

Chapter 17

January 7, 2020, Tuesday

Marley jogged down the hallway in the Emergency Department to the bay where'd she'd been told Corkie would be held. She whipped the curtain back and gasped. Corkie had a bandage on her forehead, one on her right cheek, and an impressive bruise forming under her left eye. Tubes and wires connected the teenage girl to monitors and bags of fluid overhead. For a few seconds, Marley only heard the repetitive beeping from the machines monitoring Corkie's vital signs.

The teenager opened her eyes and sent a small smile to Marley. "Hey, Dr. Bakersfield, sorry they bothered you."

She stepped to the bed and rested her hand on the girl's lower leg. "What are you talking about? Of course, I came. I had to help my best assistant. We have to keep you in top shape, so you can take the medical field by storm in a few years."

The girl pressed her hand to her sides, trying to sit up further. She grimaced.

Marley moved closer. "Hey, don't move. Stay still. I wanted to let you know I took a look at your scans and labs, and everything else looks good. You have some lacerations I'd like to attend to myself, but once those are sewn up, I think you'll be allowed to go home."

The girl smiled.

Marley lifted a warning finger. "If you promise to take it easy and rest for the next few days. And no gym class at school for a few weeks."

"Well, I won't argue with you over that point. I hate gym class. The other kids tease me about my lack of sports ability as well as my shocking white legs in the shorts they make us wear."

Marley grinned. "Okay, then we have a deal. Let me grab a surgical tray and some supplies, and I'll be right back." She darted out the room, and two hours later, she'd repaired Corkie's lacerations and redressed them. She stared at her work and gave a nod. "It will heal nicely, I think." Pulling the blue surgical gloves off one at a time, Marley tossed them in the nearby trashcan.

A dark-haired, older nurse named Nancy stuck her head into the room. "Dr. Bakersfield, uh, could I speak to you for a moment."

Frowning, Marley looked at Corkie first. "You need anything?"

The girl shook her head. "No, I'm fine. Thanks."

Marley turned and followed the nurse out the door and into the hallway.

"Why don't we find somewhere quiet to talk?" The woman led Marley to an empty patient room and shut the door behind them.

"What's going on? Another consult?"

The woman took a seat in a blue chair and pointed for Marley to sit in one as well. "Um, I got some news, Dr. Bakersfield. Some bad news, unfortunately. I know you haven't been in town long, and we don't know one another well, but I've come to appreciate your work ethic, and your patients love you. I hate to have to tell you this...you seem like a good person." The woman wrung her hands in her lap.

Marley reached forward and placed a hand on the woman's, settling them. "What is it, Nancy?"

The woman pulled in a deep breath and held it for a few seconds before releasing it. "Okay. Okay. The thing is...I got a notification...an ambulance had been called to a town residence...for a fall. I thought the address sounded familiar...I—" She cast her eyes to her lap.

Marley's heart beat faster. "Yes?"

The woman looked Marley in the eye and then glanced away before continuing, "They're bringing the patient in to follow protocol, but he was found deceased at the scene. I believe they tried

119

to resuscitate him, but…anyways, the ambulance is bringing the patient here. They wanted to notify the family and confirm the time of death. Sign paperwork."

Marley's chest burned. "Nancy, who is the patient?"

This time, she lifted her eyes to Marley and didn't look away. "It's your father. I'm sorry…he fell, hit his head, and he didn't make it. I don't know a lot more details than that. I guess his secretary stopped by the office and found him on the floor and called the ambulance."

Her throat ached, and tears brimmed to the surface of her eyes. She whispered, "No."

The woman patted her hand. "I'm so, so sorry. I believe your mother has already been called and is on her way. Is there anyone else you want me to notify?"

The image of Benjamin flashed through Marley's mind. She wanted to tell him the awful news and sob in his arms, but after the way things went this morning, she didn't think she could call him. She shook her head. "No. Could you let me know when my mother arrives?" She remembered that Jesse was supposed to meet her at the hospital probably an hour ago. She bet he sat in the waiting room. "Oh, someone might be looking for me. A guy. If he's in the waiting room, could you tell him there's been a family emergency, and I'll have to meet him later or call him. He may want to head home. His name is Dr. Sloan."

The woman nodded. "Sure thing, Dr. Bakersfield. For the record, your father made a huge difference in this community. He'll be missed." The woman crept out the door, shutting it quietly behind her.

Marley allowed all of the anguish and pain from the past to release. Sobs wracked her body, and she wrapped her arms across her chest. *How could she have left her father alone at the office? She should have driven him home.*

Thirty minutes passed, but to Marley, it could have been thirty hours. She stifled her cries and plucked several tissues from the box on the counter. Wiping her eyes, she gathered herself and took a long, shuddering breath before standing. Placing her hand on the door handle, Marley closed her eyes and asked God to help her before opening the door.

"Woah, there. Sorry, didn't see you coming." Mr. Blackstone stood in front of her, a look of surprise on his face. He obviously hadn't expected to see her.

Of all the people to run into today. "Mr. Blackstone excuse me. I have to go."

He put a hand up, pausing her exit. "Uh, Marley, I heard about your father…terrible news. And I know it isn't the ideal moment to discuss this in detail. However, I wonder if we could arrange a time to talk about the future of your father's practice?"

Rage coursed through her veins. How dare he bring this up now. She responded with a terse, "You're right. This isn't the best time to discuss the practice." She started to flee.

He jutted out his arm, blocking her way once more. "There's another matter, as well. You see, a little bird told me they saw you in the kitchen at the beginning of the bake-off. They said you used salt from the school's kitchen."

Marley wanted to scream. *What was wrong with this guy? He knew her father had died, and he wanted to discuss her usage of salt?* "So?" she spat.

"The contest had a lot riding on it, and the rules clearly state that all materials and supplies must be provided by the contestant. Taking salt from the school kitchen violates the rules. That means the entrant you supplied the salt to, Benjamin Miller, would be disqualified from the competition and lose the prize money he'd won."

A wave of nausea washed over Marley. She whispered, "No."

He gave an artificial empathetic nod. "Yes, I'm afraid…of course, there may be a solution to both problems."

She shivered. Crossing her arms, Marley hugged herself tight. "And what might that be?"

"Well, I could forget about the usage of the kitchen's ingredients in the winning entry if we could come to an understanding regarding your father's medical practice. Besides, with your father's passing, I think selling the practice and getting a good price for it would bring relief to you and your mother. It would allow you to return to your big city hospital. And Benjamin Miller could keep his money. I thought I'd heard something about him using the cash award to save the bakery. Maybe even expand it." He made a tisking sound. "Sure would be a shame for him to lose it all over a little salt."

"How could you?"

Mr. Blackstone narrowed his eyes. "I'm only doing my job, which requires me to look out for the best interest of this town and my family. I'm sure your father would have understood."

"Don't ever speak about my father again. You're nothing like him."

Shaking his head, he started to walk away, whistling. After a few steps, he stopped and spun around. "Oh, Dr. Bakersfield, don't take too long giving me an answer. From the looks of the gentleman in the waiting room, your running out of time. I think D.C. may not be as patient as me."

Marley stormed down the hall and away from the horrible man. *How could she sell her father's practice? But how could she let Benjamin lose everything?* As Marley pushed the door to the waiting room open, she realized Mr. Blackstone was right about one thing— D.C. didn't look too patient. Dr. Jesse Sloan sat in a chair opposite Benjamin Miller, and the look on both their faces could have ignited the room with a spark.

~

Benjamin shifted his glare away from Jesse at the sound of the door to the Emergency Department opening. His eyes fell upon Marley, and they softened. Even though he didn't know if he could trust her with his heart, he still had to come when he heard from Mrs. Klingensmith about Marley's father.

Marley's red-rimmed eyes looked puffy, and she held herself in a close embrace as if to protect herself from the world. She reminded him of the tormented little girl he'd known as a child. Benjamin murmured, "Marley, Mrs. Klingensmith called me... I'm so sorry."

Jesse scrunched his brow. "Sorry about what?"

Marley walked closer and spoke between short sobs, "My dad...he...he..."

"He died," Benjamin uttered.

Jesse's eyes widened, and he wore a look of genuine shock. "Oh, wow, Marley, I'm sorry...I didn't know."

She sniffled. "It just happened. While I was here. I ran into my mom in the hallway, and she said the medics thought he'd tripped on a rug in his office. He must have caught his crutch on it, and he fell. They said he hit the back of his head. He's been taking blood thinners, and they think he suffered a subdural hematoma."

The words didn't make sense to Benjamin, but he knew the pain Marley felt. He'd experienced it with the loss of his mother. He started to step forward and offer a hug.

Jesse beat him to it, though. He swung his arm across Marley's shoulder and patted her arm. "Hey, why don't you let me take you and your mom home. I have to head back to the city tonight because I'm on call tomorrow, but I'll talk to the partners for you. I'm sure they'll understand that it may take a few days or a week for you to return. That'll give you time to get things with your father's practice settled and tend to his service."

Benjamin couldn't hold his tongue, "So, you're leaving? For sure?" He couldn't believe, after everything they'd been through, all the feelings they'd shared, that she would walk away from him, her town, and her father's medical practice.

She stared at him through eyes that looked like sad pools. "I…I don't know. I need to talk—"

Marley's mother stuck her head out the door connecting the waiting room to the emergency room. "Marley, I need you. The staff is asking me questions, and I don't know what to tell them. They want to know what funeral home we plan to use, and I…I can't…I can't." Her mother started weeping.

Turning to Benjamin, Marley wore a pained expression. "I have to go." She shifted her eyes to Jesse. "Don't worry about waiting on us. We may be here a while, but I have my car. I can get us home. Fill the partners in, and I'll talk to you in a few days." Then, she dashed away to join her mother.

Benjamin shifted his weight and shoved his hands in his pockets. "I guess you might as well head back to D.C."

Dr. Sloan surveyed his competition and smirked. "Yeah, I guess so. Besides, I know Marley, and I know she won't turn her back on the practice she's built in D.C. Even after everything that happened with her father. The dust will settle here, and she'll come back to me."

Clenching his fists, Benjamin narrowed his eyes. "I know Marley, too. I've known her for a long time."

"Don't you want what's best for her? Don't you want her to succeed, to move past all the small-town drama she endured?"

Benjamin's confidence faltered. "What do you know about her small-town drama?"

"I know she didn't speak highly of this place and her past, and for whatever reason, she avoided coming home except for major holidays. Even then, she never took more than a day or two off work. I know she loves plastic surgery, and I don't think she's going to throw away her career for a baker. Do you?" He raised his brow.

Several phrases circulated through Benjamin's mind, but none of them would be considered Godly, so instead, he kept his mouth shut.

"Huh. No rebuttal. Because you know I'm right. I've got to go. Better get back to your bakery. Those scones and muffins aren't going to make themselves." Jesse Sloan sauntered away with a sure stride; his head held high.

Benjamin knew he loved Marley, and he'd thought she loved him, too. But maybe love wasn't enough. Maybe Jesse Sloan had it right, and Benjamin needed to step aside and let Marley lead the life she'd worked hard to attain. Far away from him. Far away from her hometown. Far away from all her pain. The room suddenly felt suffocating. He jogged out of the hospital and into the cold, winter air, not looking back. He'd loved her most of his life, but maybe it was time he let go of Marley Bakersfield once and for all.

Chapter 18

January 14, 2020, Tuesday

Marley packed away the last sweater into her suitcase and zipped it shut. She sat on the edge of her childhood bed and looked out the window. An unusual drizzle caused ribbons of water to stream down her bedroom window. A tear spilled over her eyelid and trickled down her cheek, and she choked back another sob.

Yesterday, she'd laid her father to rest, enduring the wake and funeral. Neighbors flooded their home after the service, dropping off condolences and food as if starvation were the problem and her pain could be fixed by a well-cooked casserole.

Although Marley and her father hadn't always gotten along, they'd come to understand one another much more over the past month. She looked around her room, feeling like a lost little girl. The pain from her childhood had started to dissipate, but since her father's death and the run-in with Mr. Blackstone, all her inadequacies flooded back.

She'd talked to her mother about the practice, and her mother agreed to sell it to Mr. Blackstone. Marley had called him to let him know, and she could almost hear him punching the air in victory. It made her sick.

A knock at the door interrupted her thoughts. "Marley, Honeybun, are you ready to go?"

Marley glanced around her bedroom. "Yeah, I think so. Are you sure you won't come with me? Even for a little while?" She'd begged her mother return to D.C. with her--to make a fresh start. She hated leaving her mother alone.

Sitting on the bed next to Marley, her mom shook her head. "No, this town is my home. I don't know what the future holds, but I know running away isn't the answer for me."

"Do you think that's what I'm doing, Mom? Running away?"

"I think you're doing what you think is the best thing for you. And I understand your reasons, but…are you sure you don't want to try to talk with Benjamin once more before you go? Maybe sort things out?"

"Mom, I…I can't. I can't do it. If I stay here any longer…I love you, and I miss Dad and don't want to let him down, but this town, this place…I feel like I can't breathe. I feel like I'm a kid again, and I've fallen off my bike and scarred up my face or walked on the bus and heard the kids teasing me or walked down the halls at Prom and face planted. I've failed. I've failed with whatever mission God gave me when I came here. And the best thing for me, you, and Benjamin is for me to leave."

Her mother looked her in the eye and gave her a sad smile. "I don't think you've failed. I think you're lost. I think you're grieving. But I don't think you've failed. You definitely haven't failed me." She gave her daughter a sidearm hug and laid her head on Marley's shoulder before rising. Turning around before leaving the room, her mother gazed at Marley. "Promise you'll call as soon as you get home? So, I know you're safe?"

"I promise."

Her mother left the room, and all the tears Marley had been holding back spilled over. *No, going to D.C. remained her only option.* She'd both received and caused too much pain since returning home. She stood up and heaved her luggage off the bed, dragging it to her car. As she loaded the last suitcase, she slammed the trunk. Hopping in the driver's seat, she turned the ignition and stared at her childhood home. Marley knew when her dad had called her to help him with the practice that she couldn't refuse him. However, Marley wondered if all the pain from the past month could have been avoided if she'd never returned to Blackstone Haven. Marley shoved her car into reverse and decided never to look back on her past again. It only led to trouble.

~

Benjamin knew Marley had left town earlier that morning. Mrs. Klingensmith had stopped by the bakery and shared the news with him first.

The door to the bakery opened, and Stacey Blackstone strolled in as if she'd won a prize. "Well, I guess you heard about Marley? Such a shame she had to head home, but that's how it is when you're a big city gal, I guess. Still, I can't believe she left her mom like that. Doesn't seem too thoughtful to me."

"Stacey you don't know what you're talking about. She was a kind person with a good heart and an excellent doctor. Marley planned to come to town for a short while, and I heard she offered to move her mother to D.C. with her, but Sally didn't want to go."

"Humph. Well, Marley must not have cared much for you if a buyout was all it took to get rid of her. If you ask me, this town and the medical community is better off without her. You know she agreed to sell her daddy's practice to my father's hospital corporation, right? The patients will be in much better hands. Plus, if she hadn't sold it, I don't know what it would have meant for you." Stacey clamped her mouth shut and immediately looked like she'd said something she shouldn't have.

Benjamin had been wiping the counter with a rag and stopped. He lifted his head and peered at Stacey. "What do you mean?"

"Well, I, uh, mean if she hadn't sold the practice, then I don't know what would have happened to your bakery. I think she made the right choice going along with my father. He can be a tough man--he always gets what he wants."

Planting his hands on the counter, Benjamin leaned forward. "And what exactly does your father want? What does it have to do with my bakery?"

Now Stacey's face flushed red. "Uh, um…"

"Stacey."

"Oh, I think my father heard from someone that Marley used an ingredient from the school's kitchen during the bake-off, which, as you know, is against the rules."

"I didn't know anything about this. However, if she did do it, she didn't know it was against the rules. I don't see what that has to do with her dad's medical practice."

"Um, well, I think daddy might have suggested that if she agreed to sell her father's practice to his hospital, which by the way is going to benefit the community and give the patient's more access to care, and really, if you think about it, benefit Marley because she can't take over her dad's practice, not with her job in D.C., so honestly it works out better for everyone all the way around and—"

Benjamin pounded a fist on the counter. "Stacey! What are you saying?"

"He suggested if she sold him her dad's practice, then he would look the other way about the contraband ingredient. That way, you'd remain the winner of the bake-off and keep the prize money." She tucked her chin and looked away.

"What?" he shouted. "He didn't."

She glanced at him again and gave a small nod.

"So, you're telling me that your father blackmailed Marley, and that's why she left the way she did?"

"None of us can be sure about her reasons for leaving…not all of them. I'm positive she would've come to the decision on her own to leave and sell the practice, Bennie. It really is the best choice for her and the community. And look," she gestured to the bakery with her hands like a game show assistant, "you get to use the money to help your business--your mom's business. So, I'd say the ends justify the means."

Benjamin's eyes widened, and his jaw fell. "You've got to be kidding me. The ends justify the means. What kind of cliché garbage is that? Your family…your family…" *Careful, Benjamin. Watch your words. There is still God to answer to, no matter what someone does. Turn the other cheek.* Right now, his pulse throbbed, and he wanted to scream. "I think you better go."

Stacey stared at him for a second, then headed toward the door.

"Oh, and Stacey," he called after her.

She paused, her hand on the door handle. Lifting her head, she pasted her fake smile back in place. "Yes?"

"Don't call me Bennie again."

She narrowed her eyes. "You would have been lucky to be the man on my arm, Benjamin Miller. You're making a huge mistake letting me go like this." She yanked the door open and stormed outside.

He ran a hand through his hair and leaned back against the counter. What a mess. He'd let Marley go... he'd let the only woman he'd ever loved leave. Benjamin pulled out his phone and found her name in his contact list. He punched the button and waited as it rang. After three rings, it went to voicemail. He didn't know what to say. "Uh, Marley, this is Benjamin. When you get this message, please call me back. It's important." Hanging up the phone, he slammed it on the counter. Benjamin couldn't let Marley give up on her dad's practice or him without a fight. But first, he had to get her to call him back.

Chapter 19

January 16, 2020, Thursday

Tara chomped on a wad of pink bubblegum and blew a bubble. It popped, and she dove into interrogating her best friend, "So, you're not going to call Benjamin back?"

Marley turned her head away, refusing to meet Tara's gaze. "Calling him back isn't going to change anything."

"You're turning your back on love for this?" Tara raised her hands, gesturing to the walls of the hospital locker room.

"You like this." Marley waved a hand in the air as she brushed a stray hair from her face with the other one.

"Yes, this place is great for me. Perfect, actually. But I remember how you sounded when you talked about Benjamin during our phone calls while you were gone. You love him. I don't see how you can turn your back on him and pretend none of it happened."

"I'm not pretending none of it happened, believe me. I feel terrible about how things ended and leaving my patients behind…I mean, my father's patients."

"Are you sure accepting the partnership and staying here is the right thing for you? Don't get me wrong, I don't know what I would do if you left, but if that's what you wanted, then I'd support you. Make sure you're choosing something and not running away from something else. Okay?" Tara stepped closer and put a hand on Marley's shoulder.

Marley looked at her best friend, and her eyes burned. She couldn't start crying. Not here at work. She thought if the tears came, they wouldn't stop. Thankfully, her phone rang, interrupting the impending torrent of tears. Pulling it out of her scrub pocket, Marley answered, "Mom? Is everything okay?"

"Everything's fine, Marley. Well, that's not true. Your father's gone, so everything is not fine. But you know what I meant."

Marley's throat tightened again. "I know," she croaked.

"Honeybun, I wanted to make sure you could come back in a few weeks to finish things with your dad's practice. There are some final forms you need to sign for Mr. Blackstone and the hospital. Do you think you could come on February 13th?"

"The day before Valentine's Day?"

"What? You have a hot date?"

Marley laughed for the first time in weeks. "No, definitely not. I guess I can do it then."

"Great. How are you doing...really?"

"Oh, I don't know, Mom. It's hard... I'm mad at myself...I should have been there for Dad. Maybe I could have prevented all of this from happening. I'm a horrible person."

Her mother sighed. "Marley, that's not true. I think you're in pain. I think you've been in pain for a long time. I think you've never felt good enough, pretty enough. But, Honeybun, I want to tell you something. You made your father so proud--and not because you're smarter than a whip, but because you're beautiful. Inside and out."

"Mom."

Her mother pressed on, "No, I mean it. I watched for years as you hid within yourself. But you don't have to hide--not anymore. Do you know your father's favorite Bible verse?"

"No."

"The verse is from 1 Samuel 16:7. The Lord does not look at the things man looks at. Man looks at the outward appearance, but the LORD looks at the heart." Most people think it means God doesn't care about outside stuff, beauty. Your father always held fast to the second part—that God looks on the heart of man; on his intentions and motives. And Honeybun, you have the best heart, the best intentions of anyone I know. That's what matters to God, and that's what mattered to your father. It's why he served in the army, it's why he asked me to marry him, and it's why he built his practice.

131

He wanted to serve God, his family, and his town. He only wanted the best for you. If you think staying in D.C. will make you happy, then I know he'd approve."

Marley stared at her reflection in the locker room mirror as her mother spoke, and more tears rose to the surface.

"But…if you change your mind…you always have a home here. Blackstone Haven, Marley, is your home. Always has been, always will be. And don't forget who you are—a beautiful, kind woman of God."

All of the tears fell, and with them, Marley's last shred of armor. "Thanks, Mom. I appreciate everything you said. And I promise to call you more. Every day, in fact."

"And you'll come back in a few weeks for the final closure of your father's estate?"

"Of course, Mom."

"And you'll come with me to the town's Valentine's Day dance?"

She frowned. "Mom."

"What? You can't expect me to go to the Valentine's Day dance by myself. As a widow. After losing my husband."

Her mom knew how to work the guilt angle. "I'll think about it." She pulled in a breath. Releasing it, Marley scanned the room. She supposed she should feel closure at the idea of returning to D.C., her job, and her best friend. But she didn't. In fact, Marley felt like she'd lost everything that mattered—her father, his practice, and Benjamin's love. No, she couldn't stay in Blackstone Haven. Everyone would be better off without her around to make a mess of everything, no matter her mother's sincere words.

Marley hung up the phone and gathered herself before exiting the locker room. She promised Tara they'd meet for coffee later in the week and left. As she walked into the hallway, she bumped into Dr. Jesse Sloan. "Oh, uh, hi. How are you?" Marley stammered.

He sent her a confident grin. "Better now that our soon-to-be newest partner of the group is back. Are you ready for the final meeting?" He raised a brow.

Her palms began to sweat. She'd tried to forget about the meeting. In a few weeks, she had to sit down with the senior members of the practice again and discuss the partnership contract's details and sign it—commit. With it being a four-year contract, she had to be sure. She'd moved the meeting once already since returning, begging off with the excuse she had a lot of work to catch up on due to her absence. The partners had accepted this excuse once, but she doubted she could weasel out of the meeting a second time without raising concern. "As ready as I can be, I suppose."

Jesse stepped closer and placed a hand on her shoulder. "I want you to know, Marley, you are making the right decision. That two-bit small-town is your past. This place, our practice, you, me, this is your future."

This was her future, huh. Her future caused her stomach to clench and bile to rise to the back of her throat. She urged it back down and forced a smile. "Thanks. Hey, I've got to run. Lots of patients to see still."

Jesse moved aside and waved her past. "Of course. I look forward to us spending more time together and making your partnership official. D.C. Marley--this is the place for you. You look like you belong here. I bet Blackstone Haven doesn't even know about injectables."

"Maybe not, but Jesse, you know that's not all we do, right?"

"Maybe you don't, but for me, I'm looking to push my part of the practice toward high-paying cash-only medical procedures."

"That's not what I want, though…I want to provide great plastic surgery care for underserved patients. I want to fix cleft palates and offer cosmetic repairs that make patients feel better about themselves. I want to help—to make a difference. It's not about the money for me."

"That's great, Marley. Say all of that to the other partners, and you are in for sure."

She frowned. "But that's honestly how I feel."

"It's gold, I'm telling you. Well, I've got to run, too. Don't worry, you have a bright future here. You'll make more money than you could imagine as a partner, and we'll have some fun along the way."

She thought she saw dollar signs in his eyes.

Jesse spun around and walked away, his hands in his pockets.

Marley didn't know what to do, but she knew she didn't want to become another Dr. Jesse Sloan. A second wave of nausea washed over her, and she hurried down the hallway to round on her patients.

Whatever happened in the coming weeks, Marley needed to figure her life out—quick.

~

Marley spent the next few weeks alternating between long hours at the hospital and crashing for a couple of hours at home before returning to work. She hoped to distract herself from the upcoming meeting with the partners and the decision she had before her.

She stood before the locker room mirror and pulled her hair back into a low ponytail. After smoothing her bangs to the side, ensuring her scar remained hidden, she stared at herself. Her phone rang, and she looked at it. She didn't recognize the number. "Hello, this is Dr. Bakersfield."

"Dr. Bakersfield... it's Corkie. From Blackstone Haven? I'm sorry to bother you..." Marley's shoulders relaxed. "Corkie you aren't bothering me. How are you doing?"

"I'm great. I heard from Mrs. Klingensmith that you were coming back to town for the Valentine's Day dance."

"Well, I'm coming to sign some papers the day before. My mom wants me to go to the dance with her. I haven't decided for sure if I'm going to it. Why?"

"Oh, I wanted to thank you...in person. I have a small gift for you. My face healed well, and you can hardly see the scars. You don't know how grateful I am that you came to the hospital to take care of me. I wanted to call sooner to thank you, but after everything that happened with your dad...I didn't know if you'd want to hear from me."

"That's crazy, Corkie. Why wouldn't I want to hear from my best assistant?"

"I thought you might blame me for...well, for your dad. I'm so, so sorry, Dr. Bakersfield. I wish you had stayed with him. It's my fault you came to the hospital."

"No, Corkie, don't say that... it's not your fault he died. Dr. Walter Bakersfield couldn't be told anything—he was a stubborn man. Even if I'd stayed at the office with him, he still might have fallen and hit his head. You couldn't help it."

"Yeah, but I shouldn't have been in the car that wrecked. I got in because all the other kids were taking turns racing one another and Chelsea said I was a chicken, and no way would I do a ride-along. I can't believe I made such a dumb decision. If I hadn't worn my seatbelt, I'd probably be dead. Anyway, I wanted to thank you for taking care of me and tell you I'm done with worrying about what those high school kids think. Someday, I'm going to be a strong female doctor like you, and I'm going to change the world."

Marley blinked her eyes, and fresh tears fell. "Thank you, Corkie."

"No, thank you, Dr. Bakersfield. You are the most wonderful person I know. See you soon." The girl hung up the phone.

Marley had never felt more special. Even if she didn't do anything else right in her life, she'd made a difference to Corkie. Marley realized what she had to do but wanted to talk to Tara first. Glancing at her phone, she pressed the button to connect her to Tara.

Her friend answered, "Hello?"

"Hey, do you have a minute?"

Snapping her gum, Tara gave a casual, "Yeah, girl, what's up?"

Marley stared straight ahead at her reflection. *Who did she want to be for the rest of her life? Scarly Marley or Dr. Marley Bakersfield?* "I need your help with something."

More chomping. "You got it."

"I'm going to my meeting tonight with Dr. Fortwright, Dr. Thomas, and Dr. Sloan, and I'm turning down the partnership."

Marley could almost hear Tara's jaw hit the floor. "No way."

"Yes way. And there's more."

"Besides totally imploding your flashy career?"

"Hey, I thought you were on my side."

"I'm kidding. I'm always on your side. But this is a big deal. If you aren't going to take the partnership here, then what are you going to do?"

"I'm heading back to Blackstone Haven, and I'm taking over my father's practice. I'll run it as a dual board-certified general and plastic surgeon. If you decide you need a break from the big city, then I can add pediatrics to the list."

"Wow, that's a major decision. Are you sure?"

She gazed at the scar on her forehead, and her mother's words echoed in her mind. *God looks on the heart.* She recognized what her heart held. "Yes, I'm sure. But there's more. This is the part I need your help because I don't know if I can do it on my own."

"I'm in," Tara affirmed.

"I'll have to confront Mr. Blackstone. He's not going to like me keeping the medical practice, and he's probably going to try to threaten to take away the prize money from Benjamin. That's where you come in."

"What do I have to do with you and the baker?"

"We're attending the Valentine's Day dance, and I'm going to tell Benjamin how I feel. I'll take the stage and tell everyone in the town about how Mr. Blackstone tried to blackmail me. I realize it still might put Benjamin's title at risk, but at least the public will know the truth about the Mr. Blackstone. He can't continue to treat people like this: him or his daughter. I'm taking a stand--for my dad, for Benjamin, and for that little girl who fell off her bike all those years ago. I'm tired of hiding behind my bangs."

"What? What are you talking about? What do bangs have to do with this?"

"It's a metaphor, Tara. Come on, follow along with me, here."

"So, what do you need me for then?"

"I need you to come for moral support and to provide a distraction to Mr. Blackstone and possibly Stacey if she shows up at the dance. I figure when I don't sign the paperwork handing the practice over, it's going to set off alarm bells for Mr. Blackstone. I might need you to keep him occupied until I have a chance to talk to Benjamin. I don't want to blindside him with all of this. It's going to be putting his prize money on the line. I'm hoping the town will understand and want him to still have it, but you never know."

~

As Marley stood outside the conference room door, ready to attend the meeting with the plastic surgery partners to sign her contract, her hands shook. Marley breathed in and exhaled. Even though she knew what she needed to do, it didn't make it any easier. Placing her hand on the door handle, she turned it and entered the room.

"Dr. Bakersfield, good to see you. It's great to have you back from the country. I haven't seen you much since your return. I was beginning to think you'd decided to stay in…what was the name of that little town?"

"Dr. Fortwright, Dr. Thomas, Dr. Sloan," she nodded to each of them, "good to see you all, too. Thanks for covering for me while I was away. Blackstone Haven. That's where I went. My hometown."

Dr. Thomas nodded. "Right, I think Dr. Sloan mentioned that now that you say it. Sorry to hear about your father. Terrible news."

She walked to the table and pulled out a chair, sinking into it. "Thank you. Yes, it was terrible."

"Well, I think I speak for the group when I say we all extend our condolences."

Dr. Fortwright shuffled papers in front of him. "I hate to jump right into this, but I've got dinner plans, and I believe Dr. Thomas has a late case tonight, so we should get to it."

She turned her attention to Dr. Thomas. "Of course. I wanted to discuss with you all——"

Dr. Sloan interjected, "How excited you are to be joining the leadership of such an illustrious practice? You've made the right choice by returning."

Dr. Thomas snapped his head toward Marley. "Had you considered not coming back to D.C.?"

She shifted in her seat and fiddled with a button on her white coat. "That's what I wanted to speak with you all about today. You see…going home taught me some important things…about myself…but also about what I want for my life."

Dr. Sloan frowned. "I thought you wanted this."

She nodded and continued, "Yes, I did. But, being home, well, it was hard at first. However, I realized I'm a different person than I was twenty years ago. I'm different than even a year ago. Blackstone Haven needs me. My father's practice needs me. And there is someone who captured my heart…, and I believe he needs me. God showed me a lot about what I want and need, and respectfully, I don't think staying in D.C. is it."

Dr. Sloan's mouth dropped open. "Are you serious? You're throwing away your career. You know that?"

She shook her head. "I don't see it that way, but I understand what you're saying." She looked at Dr. Thomas and then Dr. Fortwright. "Thank you for the opportunity. I'm sorry to inform you of my decision at such a late date, but I didn't realize what I wanted until recently. I hope you understand."

Dr. Thomas cast a knowing glance at Dr. Fortwright before speaking, "I had a feeling when you left you might not come back. I can't say I'm surprised. You've always had a big heart, and while our practice offers a lot of charitable cases, I can see the appeal of small-town medicine. I can't say I think you're making the best decision for your career, but it sounds like you've weighed your options and know what you want." He rose and extended a hand to her. "Thank you for your time. Your contract will end on January 30th, and per your request today, we won't be renewing it. I wish you the best in your future endeavors."

Marley smiled and stood. She shook his hand. "Thank you, sir." Turning to the other partners, Marley offered her hand to them. Dr. Fortwright accepted, but Dr. Sloan sat, staring at her, shock splattered across his face. She didn't want to get into a confrontation with him, so she excused herself and left the room quickly.

Once in the hallway, Marley leaned against the wall. She released the breath she'd held for the duration of the meeting. *One hard thing completed.* Now, she needed to pack up her home and finish her remaining cases. With about two weeks remaining until the end of the month, it didn't leave much time to get everything done. At least she could count on Tara's help. Marley closed her eyes.

A man cleared his throat. "I can't believe you blew up your life like that."

Marley opened her eyes and turned to face the speaker. "Jesse...you don't understand. I'm not the same person as when I left. I know what I want, and I know what I'm doing."

"But what about career advancement? What about financial security? What about us?" He frowned.

Marley thought she saw genuine hurt in his eyes. She whispered kindly, "There never was an 'us,' and I don't care about the money. I want to go home and take care of my mom and my town. Going back to Blackstone Haven...well, it was the scariest thing I've ever done. I've tried to hide from my past my entire life, but confronting it felt freeing, Jesse. I'm not the timid little girl from my childhood. I'm strong and capable, and I know God is looking at my heart. My heart wants to serve Him, and I believe He wants me to take over my father's practice and make sure his patients get the best care. I'm not letting Mr. Blackstone take away my father's legacy…my legacy. I hope you understand."

He shrugged. "I can't say I understand, but it sounds like you're settled on it. For the record, I think it's a mistake."

She sent him a sad smile. "I know you do. Thank you for your concern. I hope you'll be happy, Jesse. I've got to go. Lots to do before I leave." She gave him a small wave, hurrying down the hall away from the past and toward her bright future. She hoped.

Chapter 20

February 13, 2020, Thursday

Marley looked at Tara and sighed. "It's not going to work. All this stuff is not going to fit in the car. It's not humanly possible."

Tara plopped on the bed, causing it to bounce. She grinned. "Ah, but you're forgetting something."

"And what's that?"

"That you have help..." Tara gestured to herself. "Me. I'm coming with you for the first few days to get you through Valentine's Day and dodging the any Mr. Blackstone's attacks. I'll toss some of your stuff in my car. After all, I only need one bag." Tara peered around the bedroom, now covered with duffel bags, suitcases, and trash bags. With most of Marley's household and personal items packed away, the space looked stark and empty. "I still can't believe you're moving."

Marley sent her friend a half-grin. "I know, but it's only a few hours away. You can visit me anytime. You'll always have a place to crash, and I promise to come back and see you, too. Plus, there's girl's weekends. I'm sure we can come up with a few tropical locations to vacation at throughout the year."

Tara nodded. "I know. But it's not the same. It's the end of an era."

Moisture filled Marley's eyes.

Tara noticed her friend's tears, and she stood to give Marley a hug. As Tara squeezed her friend, she spoke into Marley's ear, "But the beginning of another one. A new era. A new beginning. And it's going to be great. I'm so, so proud of you and happy for you. You deserve the best." She released her friend and scanned the room. "So, did we get it all packed?"

Marley looked around the room a final time. "I think so. We need to get these last few bags in the cars, but then I'm good to go." She picked up a duffel bag and grabbed the handle of the largest suitcase. Turning to her friend, she raised a brow. "You really think Benjamin will take me back? Not that we were officially together, but you know what I mean."

Tara gave a firm nod. "Yes. We aren't considering any other alternative. Now, come on, let's go. We need to get you started on your new life."

Heading to her car, Marley dragged several bags with her. After an hour of shoving things into every available nook, she hopped in the car. Driving away, she said a silent goodbye to her past and a hopeful hello to her future.

~

Benjamin sat at his desk in the storage room of his bakery, staring at the account ledger. He rolled his sleeves up and stretched his arms overhead, releasing a sigh. Gratitude filled his heart. With the prize money from the bake-off, he'd be able to pay off the bakery's debts his mother accrued years ago. Despite his business acumen, he'd not been able to dig out of the hole she had created. His mother had a generous spirit and gave away as many items as she sold. He should have enough left over to expand, and he couldn't have done it without Marley.

His eyes drifted to the calendar hanging on the wall. February 13th. He'd heard from the Blackstone Haven rumor mill that Marley had an appointment with Mr. Blackstone today. It pained him to think of her selling her dad's medical practice. He doubted she'd stay in town long—she was probably anxious to get back to her big-city life. He wondered if she had a big city boyfriend now, too. Since the funeral, he hadn't talked to Marley's mom to find out any more information.

Benjamin folded his hands together to pray. "God, help me know what to do. I don't want to get my heart broken again. Give me a sign if I should go after her."

He opened his eyes, and they settled on his verse-of-the-day calendar on the edge of his desk. He hadn't turned it over yet for today. As he flipped the page, his hand froze. It read, "God looks on the heart." *What was in his heart?* He loved Marley and wanted to spend the rest of his life with her. He'd loved her since they were kids. Also, he didn't want to see her get hurt, which is what he thought selling her father's practice would do. Plus, he didn't trust Mr. Blackstone. *At all.* He knew what to do. He didn't know where she'd planned to meet Mr. Blackstone, but he had a guess, and he hoped it would be right. "Thank you, God," he whispered.

Rising from his seat, he grabbed his jacket off the back of his chair and hurried out of the bakery, flicking off lights as he left. He jammed his keys in the front door lock and ran for his car. If he hurried, he might make it. He might be able to stop her from selling. He might be able to save their relationship. The one thing Benjamin Miller knew for sure—he had to try. He clenched his jaw and yanked his car door open, practically leaping into the seat. The roar of the engine mirrored the burning in his heart for Marley as he drove to the Dr. Bakersfield Surgical Practice.

~

Marley sat at the mahogany desk in her father's office across from Mr. Blackstone.

He leaned back in his seat and crossed one leg over the other, resting his foot on his knee. "I'm glad you came to your senses about your father's practice. You're making the best decision for him, his patients, and your family."

She smiled and folded her hands in her lap, sitting up straighter. "You know, I couldn't agree with you more. I've reviewed the documents, and after careful consideration, I've made a decision."

"Best decision of your life."

"I think so… I've decided to decline your purchase offer on my father's medical practice. I'm going to move here and take over the practice myself. I believe I can make a difference in the community and provide excellent care, and I know it's what my father would want, too. I've already spoken with my mother, and she signed over the practice to me. She agrees with the decision. All that's left to do is inform the hospital, but I wanted to let you know first."

His portly abdomen heaved with labored breaths, tugging at the buttons on his blue dress shirt. His face flew past crimson and straight into eggplant territory. Marley didn't know someone could turn that shade of color and still be breathing. He remained silent.

"Mr. Blackstone? Did you hear what I said."

He leaned forward and slammed his fist on the desk.

Marley jumped.

"Oh, I heard it all right. And I won't stand for it. Now, young lady, we had a deal. You were going to sell this practice to me and my hospital, and I was going to forget about your little mistake during the bake-off. I'd hate to have to take back the prize money from Mr. Miller."

Shoulders tense, Marley tried to take a breath before responding, "I understand you are upset. That still doesn't change my decision. Regarding Mr. Miller...I don't think the town, or the Chamber of Commerce will view my 'mistake' the way you do. I think they'll understand it was a minor error that didn't affect the outcome of the competition and will approve him to keep the check."

Bolting upright, Mr. Blackstone glared at her. "We'll see about that. This isn't over. Not by a longshot. I'm going to talk to my lawyers today. And good luck with the hospital. You may find getting credentialing and privileges more difficult this time around." With his final threat, he spun on his heel and shot out the door.

Marley exhaled and started to cry. Not from sadness or fear...but from relief. *Hurdle number two conquered.* She glanced at her father's medal, hanging on the wall and smiled. Her dad would be proud of how she stood up to the bully of a man. "He's not going to win, Dad. I promise."

Pulling out her phone from her purse, she called Tara. "Hey, I did it."

"How'd it go?"

"About as well as expected. And by that, I mean horribly, but at least it's done. I'm heading home now. Will you let my mom know?"

"Sure. She's standing here next to me. I think she mentioned something about baking three different cakes to celebrate." Tara lowered her voice, "Doesn't she know you don't eat sugar?"

Marley shook her head. Her mother would never change. But maybe that was okay. "She knows. It's fine. Tell her I'm on my way."

She rose from her seat and slung her bag over her shoulder, walking toward the office door. She hit the light switch and headed down the empty hallway. Her footsteps pounded along with her heartbeat. *Now the real work began. The start of something new. And a chance to make things right with Benjamin. Tomorrow.* Turning the light off as she left, Marley locked the door behind her, heading home.

~

Benjamin pulled into the empty parking lot of the Dr. Bakersfield Surgical Practice and turned his car off. Maybe someone had dropped her off...maybe she was inside. Or perhaps she met Mr. Blackstone at the hospital or his office or anywhere else in this town.

Stepping out of the car, he slammed the door and stared at the practice's front door. *What if Marley didn't want to talk to him? What if she no longer shared his feelings?* He shook his head--he couldn't think like that. He had to try. He ambled up the stairs to the front door and knocked. No answer. He knocked again. This time the inside lock clicked, and the door swung open.

Mrs. Klingensmith stood on the other side of the open door wearing her standard cardigan and a matching pink skirt. Her wire-rim glasses had slipped down her nose, and she pushed them up, giving him a good once over. "Benjamin Miller, what are you doing here?"

"Uh," he stammered, "I...I was looking for Dr. Bakersfield. I heard she'd returned to town, and I had hoped I'd catch her. Is she here?" He raised his brow.

She crossed her arms and sent him a knowing look. "She left about five minutes ago. You just missed her. Anything I can do for you?"

Benjamin's shoulders sagged. His efforts had been too late. She'd probably already signed away the practice to Mr. Blackstone along with any hope of a future for her in Blackstone Haven. He shook his head. "No, thank you, Mrs. Klingensmith. I didn't think anyone was here. Your car isn't in the parking lot."

She frowned. "Oh, that. My silly husband...such a worrywart. He doesn't like me to drive in the rain, dark, or snow...really any situation other than a clear day at eight in the morning. He absolutely insisted on driving me and dropping me off, but he should be here any minute to pick me up. Dr. Bakersfield told me not to come in today, but I didn't want her to face Mr. Blackstone alone."

He hung his head and stared at his scuffed and flour-covered shoes. "So, I guess that's it, then. She sold the practice to Blackstone and the hospital, and that's the end of it." He shoved his hands in his pockets and kicked at a pebble on the porch.

"What are you talking about? Haven't you been in touch with Marley? Didn't she tell you?"

Benjamin's head snapped upward. "Tell me what? I haven't spoken to her since the day of her father's funeral."

Mrs. Klingensmith's eyes widened. "Oh, well, I've never been one to stick my nose where it doesn't belong, and this is big news, so I think you should talk to her yourself."

"Mrs. Klingensmith, please. What's going on?"

She moved her fingers across her lips as if closing them with a zipper. "Nope, I've been accused of being the town gossip for the last time. You'll have to ask her."

He heaved an exaggerated sigh. "In that case, do you know where Marley is? The hospital? Her house? Back to D.C.?"

The older woman shook her head. "I'm afraid I don't know. I could give her a call if you'd like?"

He waved away her offer. "No, don't do that. I don't want to bother her. If she'd wanted me to know, I'd think she would have told me. Thanks, Mrs. Klingensmith. I'd better go." He turned around and started down the steps, feeling all the joy he'd carried earlier over the rescue of the bakery slip away with his defeat.

"Oh, Benjamin, I had a thought."

He stopped and spun around. "Yeah?" The wind picked up, carrying the sharp scent of pine and snow. He shivered.

"I believe I overhead Marley, I mean, Dr. Bakersfield, say she planned to attend the town's Valentine's Day dance tomorrow. I don't know what your plans are for the holiday, but if you want to see her, you might want to come."

Benjamin ran a hand through his hair. "The Valentine's Day dance, huh?"

She raised her arms in the air, palms upward, and shrugged. "It's a suggestion. I can't think of a better day or a better time to tell someone how you feel about them. But what do I know? I've only been married for over forty years." She winked.

He smiled and gave a small nod. "Noted. Thanks, Mrs. Klingensmith. I'll think about it. I appreciate your advice."

She waved his thanks away. "Oh, honey, that's what I do. Now, you better scoot. My husband will be here any minute, and he and I have a bet about how long I can stay out of the townspeople's business. If he sees you here talking to me, he's going to assume I'm meddling. Which I'm not."

Benjamin chuckled. "No, not you. Never. Thanks again. Maybe I'll see you tomorrow at the dance." He turned and walked to his car, sliding into the seat. He waved goodbye to the motherly woman on the porch and then drove away. For once, he could honestly say he didn't mind Mrs. Klingensmith's meddling. Maybe she knew best, and tomorrow would provide the opportunity to tell Marley how he felt. Despite Marley's likely decision to sell the practice. Perhaps she'd stay and make a fresh start with him. *Tomorrow.*

Chapter 21

February 14, 2020, Friday

Marley walked back and forth across the floor. Mrs. Klingensmith had told Marley's mother that Benjamin planned to attend the Valentine's Day dance. Ever since Marley learned this piece of information, she couldn't stop pacing.

Before she ran a rut in the floor, Marley paused. She stood in front of the mirror in her childhood bathroom, inspecting her hair. *What to do with it?* The never-ending debate. She preferred to wear it down, but then she risked her bangs shifting and exposing her scar. Pulling it back enabled her to secure her bangs, so the spot remained hidden, but she didn't like how her hair looked in a ponytail or updo as much. And they hurt her head.

Come on, Marley. This is the start of a new beginning, a chance to break free. Be bold. Wear the hair down. She nodded at her reflection, mustering confidence she didn't know she had and ran a wide-tooth comb through her hair. A few twists with a curling iron accented her natural curls, and her red waves fell down her back like a waterfall. *Who was this person unafraid to try new things? Maybe she'd even eat some sugar.* Looking at herself, she shook her head. *Let's not get too crazy.*

She did one last fluff of the roots of her hair and touched up her lip gloss. "Hey Tara, can you come here for a sec?"

Tara walked into the bathroom and grinned at Marley in the mirror. "You look great! I like your hair down. You should wear it that way more often. Well, maybe not at the hospital, since loose hair inside of wounds is usually frowned upon, but everywhere else—yes."

Arching a brow, Marley turned. "You really think it looks okay? You can totally see my scar if I move my hair behind my ear or move certain ways. Even with makeup on it." She scrunched her nose.

Tara stepped closer. "All I see is my beautiful, confident best friend ready to follow her heart and God. You've got this." She scanned Marley's outfit. "Uh, you're not wearing that tonight, are you?"

Picking up a loose cotton ball from the countertop, Marley threw it at Tara. "Funny. And, no. I'm not wearing sweatpants and a t-shirt to the Valentine's Day dance. I have a dress hanging up in my bedroom. I didn't want to wrinkle it before we left, so I need to step into it and my heels, then I'm all set."

Clapping her hands, Tara pleaded, "Come on, come on. Show me. I didn't see what you ended up choosing. The last time we discussed your dress options for tonight, you'd narrowed it down to not going at all and wearing an uptight-looking suit. I thought you'd skip out on the dance or run a business meeting. Those were the choices. So, what did you land on?"

"For your information, Smarty-pants, I found this at a little boutique down the road from my place in D.C. before we left. I forgot to tell you about it." She whisked out a floor-length red gown with a sash at the waist from within a white garment bag, hanging it on the back of her bedroom door. "What do you think?"

Now jumping up and down, Tara resembled a kid on Christmas. "I love it, I love it, I love it. It's perfect."

Marley stared at the dress again. She'd debated her selection since purchasing it, but when she tried it on in the store, the shop owner couldn't stop swooning over it, so Marley bought it. "You don't think a red dress on Valentine's Day is too…cliché?"

Tara shook her head. "Absolutely not. It's exactly the right thing to wear tonight. It's bold, it screams love and romance, and it will look gorgeous with your hair. I can't wait to see the dress on you—go put it on." She shoved her best friend into the bathroom to change.

"Okay, okay. You don't have to push. I'm going." Ten minutes later, Marley wore her new red gown, three-inch black heels, and the first genuine smile of the day. She stepped out of the bathroom to show the final result to her best friend.

Tara stood near the door, dressed in a black knee-length gown, tapping her foot.

"Sorry, it took so long. I didn't want to trip."

"Not a problem. You look amazing. The dress is perfect, but if we don't leave right now, we're going to miss the whole thing."

Marley glanced at the time on her nightstand alarm clock. *Yikes, —7:00 p.m. The dance started...well...now.* She didn't want to miss her chance to speak with Benjamin or, worse, have him show up at the dance and then leave before she even arrived. "You're right. Let's go." Marley retrieved her keys from the dresser.

Tara reached out her hand. "Hand them over."

"Why? I can drive."

"Not tonight. You've got a lot on your mind, and the last thing we need is a distracted driver. I'll drive. You review what you're going to say to Blackstone and Benjamin. Leave the chauffeuring to me."

Staring at her friend, she held the keys over Tara's hand before releasing them. "Fine. You win. But I'm not letting you control the sound system. Music selection remains part of my domain."

A wide grin spread across Tara's face. "Deal."

Marley followed Tara to the car and hopped in, trying to take her friend's advice. She reviewed the words she'd prepared in her mind. Praying over them in her heart on the way to the dance, Marley exhaled slowly. For the first time ever, she had a new feeling as she drove toward her high school—hope.

~

Marley arrived at the Valentine's Day dance and gulped. *This was it.* She pushed open the car door, stepped out, and smoothed her gown. Darting her eyes toward Tara over the top of the car, she hissed, "I'm freaking out. I know I'm a physician, and I've learned and grown, and all that stuff, but right now, at this moment, I'm. Freaking. Out."

Tara stared evenly at her. "Take a deep breath and let it out. It's going to be okay. I'm with you, God's with you. You can do this. Everything will work out—I know it. I believe it."

Obeying her friend, Marley inhaled and exhaled. She rolled her shoulders back and gave a nod. "Okay, yes. You're right. A momentary lapse of sanity. I'm good now."

"Good. Now let's start the rest of your life. First up—Mr. Blackstone."

Marley's eyes narrowed. "Mr. Blackstone." She marched through the high school's front door, and this time she didn't falter. No thoughts of tripping, falling, or otherwise embarrassing herself graced her mind. This time, she walked with confident steps, her head high, ready to face her fears and insecurities; to stand up for what was right.

As Marley entered the gymnasium where the town had held the bake-off, she surveyed the room looking for Mr. Blackstone.

He stood in the middle of the room hobnobbing with other hospital administrators, chamber of commerce leaders, and various townspeople. She approached him with a smile planted on her face. "Mr. Blackstone. Good to see you. I wonder if I might have a word with you. Alone?"

He chortled, but the levity didn't meet his eyes. "Why, Dr. Bakersfield, of course. Ladies and gentlemen, if you'll excuse us, I need to speak with Dr. Bakersfield. Can I catch up with you all in a little while? Why don't you enjoy the food and punch? I've heard the Chamber's Events Committee outdid itself this year." He shook a few hands and waved as the group dismantled before turning to face Marley. His eyes darkened. "Have you realized your mistake, Dr. Bakersfield? Had a change of heart and decided to do the right thing."

Crossing her arms in front of her chest, she met his gaze, not backing down. "You mean to tell the town how you tried to blackmail me and threatened to take away Benjamin's prize money?"

"I don't think you realize who you're dealing with, Dr. Bakersfield."

She shifted her weight, keeping her eyes on his. "Oh, I think I do. My father shared a lot of stories with me upon my return to Blackstone Haven. One of them, I recall, related to his medal on the wall in his office. I believe you might know something about that…it certainly explained a lot about how Stacey treated me my entire life and how you treated my family. However, God calls me to forgive as He has forgiven me, so I'm going to forgive you for all the wrong you've done."

He glared at her. "Very kind of you."

"Oh, I'm not doing it for kindness… I'm doing it because I've learned that beauty lies within, and God looks on the heart and cares about one's intentions, and my intentions are to align with His. However, that doesn't mean I'm going to continue to be a doormat."

His face flushed, and he lowered his voice, "I'm going to make sure Benjamin loses that bakery." He raised a finger in the air. "I think you'd be wise to—"

Tara appeared at Marley's side and interlocked her arm in Marley's. "There you are, Marley. I've been looking for you everywhere." She glanced at Mr. Blackstone and extended her hand. "Nice to meet you, sir. I'm Tara Madding, Marley's best friend and pediatrician extraordinaire. I'm only visiting for a few days, but I promised to return often, and who knows? Maybe I'll move here one day. Say, I heard your family practically built the town. Why don't you tell me everything you know about Blackstone Haven? Don't leave anything out."

"Tara, it looks like you and Mr. Blackstone have a lot to discuss. I'm going to take care of something else." She stared at Mr. Blackstone again. "And Mr. Blackstone, it's been…informative." Okay, she'd have to apologize to God. She didn't keep her cool as well as she'd have liked, but at least she hadn't said anything hateful. Marley thought her father would've approved.

~

Benjamin saw Marely from across the room. She looked stunning, and his chest pounded. He'd been making his way to her for several minutes. Various townspeople stopped and congratulated him on his bake-off win or wanted to book him for a catering gig. After his third conversation with Mr. Klingensmith, he excused himself and weaved through the crowd.

She caught his eyes, and smiled, but then looked away.

He started to wave to get her attention but didn't think it would be too smooth. Not that he wasn't beyond throwing smooth and charm out at this point. As he raised his arm to signal her, she began a conversation with Mr. Blackstone. The interaction looked tense, and for a moment, Benjamin thought he might have to come to her rescue. To her credit, she must have handled it herself because Mr. Blackstone wore an angry but befuddled expression. Another woman appeared, distracting Mr. Blackstone and freeing up Marley.

Benjamin tucked his head down and focused on closing the space between them before anyone else could interrupt. When he finally made it to her, and all the words he'd prepared to say vanished. Opening his mouth, he took in her appearance, and his heart caught in his throat. She looked lovely. More than that. She appeared radiant…and confident. He stared into her eyes and felt like he could swim in the emerald pools. "Marley, I—"

Inching forward, Marley placed a hand on his forearm. "No, let me speak first, please. I have something important to tell you. A few things, actually." She sent him a smile.

"Okay, go ahead. You first, then." He sent her an encouraging grin.

"I did something bad…at the time, I didn't know it was bad…but it turns out, I shouldn't have done it." She looked up to his eyes.

He gave a slight frown. "Marley, I know you didn't do anything wrong, I—"

She lifted her hand, interrupting him. "No, I did. Remember, at the bake-off, when I couldn't find an ingredient?"

He rubbed his jaw with his hand. "Yeah, you couldn't find the salt or something, right?"

"Right. And remember how I left for a few minutes?"

He tilted his head, trying to recall all the events of that day. "I can't say that I do. The day blurred past with all the baking and then the ceremony announcing the winner. But, Marley, listen, I know--"

She shook her head. "I have to tell you this. It's important." Her eyes darted to the floor.

Benjamin put both hands on Marley's shoulders. "Marley look at me."

She raised her head and met his gaze. "The thing is...I couldn't find the salt, so I went to the school's kitchen because I figured they had to have some. I didn't know it was against the competition rules, or I never would have taken it." She frowned. "Someone must have seen me in there and told Mr. Blackstone. He said if I didn't sell my dad's medical practice to him and the hospital, he'd disqualify you from the competition and take back the prize money. You needed that money--I couldn't stand the thought of you losing your mother's bakery. I know you'd thought about leaving in the past, but watching you work there, I could tell how much it meant to you."

He stared at her. Even though Stacey had already told him as much, Benjamin still couldn't believe what Blackstone had done. *That's not true.* He believed it, but it seemed like a low move even for him. He clenched his jaw, and his eyes narrowed. He could feel his face growing hot.

Marley's face pinched. She lifted a hand and started to place it on his chest but paused and put it back at her side. "Are you mad? You're mad at me, right? I know it was a thoughtless thing to do, but I promise, I didn't know it went against the rules. And besides, it's a silly rule. I mean, it's only salt."

Benjamin leaned in and whispered, "Stop blaming yourself. You're right—it's a silly rule. It's not your fault--you didn't know. Blackstone is not a nice guy. I came to the medical practice yesterday to stop you from selling the practice. I'm sorry that I was too late. I know you want to live in D.C. and have this big, fancy practice, but I hate to think of you handing your dad's practice over to Blackstone--at least not yet. I wanted to make sure you took your time and had all the information."

She stood before him, her eyes widened and glistening with tears. "And what information is that?"

He caressed her cheek with his hand. "I love you. I've loved you forever. Since we were kids. I always thought you were the most beautiful girl in the world. I didn't want you to sell the practice and return to D.C. until you knew I loved you. And I want us to be together."

She rested her cheek in his hand and closed her eyes for a second before opening them again. "I'm so happy to hear you say that. Can you wait here for a minute?"

He frowned, confused. "Uh, sure." He'd told her he still loved her and wanted to spend his life with her, and she was…running away? *Not a good sign.* He watched as she sauntered away and wondered if he'd laid his heart bare only to have it crushed.

~

Marley took the steps to her high school stage and drew in a deep breath. Her heart raced. *Benjamin still loved her. He wanted to be with her.* It was the best news she'd heard in a long time. She walked to the center of the stage, where a band stood in the background consisting of a keyboardist, drummer, singer, and guitarist. She nodded to them and walked up to the singer. Whispering in his ear a quick question, she hoped he'd oblige.

Nodding his head, he agreed.

Walking up to the microphone in the center of the stage, Marley grabbed ahold of it. She tapped it to see if the mic had been turned on, and the taps echoed throughout the room.

All the partygoers turned their attention toward her.

She spoke with a wavering voice into the mic, "Uh, hello. Hi. I'm Dr. Marley Bakersfield…I know most of you know my father and me. I won't take much of your time tonight, but I have something important to share with you this evening."

The room fell quiet except for the occasional clink of a glass.

Marley scanned the room, and her eyes found Mrs. Klingensmith, who gave her a wave, and her mother, who sent her a smile. She saw Tara standing next to Mr. Blackstone, who looked like his head might explode. Continuing to survey the faces, Marley ended by staring into Benjamin's eyes.

Benjamin's brow furrowed, and he looked uncertain.

She grinned at him, and his countenance relaxed a bit. She cleared her throat. "So, uh, I wanted to let you, the town of Blackstone Haven, know something that happened. Something I didn't think should go unnoticed. My father always fought for what was right and pursued honor, integrity, and Godliness. My mom reminded me how important our intentions are and how God looks upon our hearts, not our outward appearance. Not beauty. Not fake smiles. Not hearty handshakes. I struggled with understanding this all my life until recently. I didn't feel good enough, pretty enough, and growing up, I didn't think I was worthy because my outside had a flaw. Or many flaws. And even though I concealed some imperfections, it didn't fix the real problem—how I saw myself and my heart."

Several people in the crowd nodded sympathetically and murmured.

"And that's what matters-what's in our hearts. After my father's death, I was informed that if we didn't sell the medical practice, then Benjamin Miller would lose the prize money and title from the bake-off."

Several gasps echoed around the room.

"Mr. Blackstone told me he found out I had used an ingredient from the school kitchen, and it violated the bake-off rules. Now, I didn't do this violation on purpose, and if I'd known, I'd never have done it. But there you have it…I made a mistake. He wanted to use that mistake to hurt someone I loved. Someone I still love."

Benjamin's eyes widened, and a grin erupted across his face.

She reciprocated his smile before continuing, "When I left Blackstone Haven, I had no plan to return, other than to visit my mom. In fact, I even tried to convince her to leave and come to D.C. with me. She didn't want to sell the medical practice, but she didn't want me to live my father's dream. My mom wanted me to have my own dream. And at the time, I thought becoming a partner at my plastic surgery practice in D.C. was the dream. After spending some time away from here and talking with my mom, my best friend, and God, I've realized something—this town, my father's practice, and a life with Benjamin Miller… that's my dream."

Benjamin stood beaming now and took several steps closer to the stage.

The crowd started talking, the whispers growing into a roar, and many of people glared at Mr. Blackstone.

Mr. Blackstone strode toward her, bounding up the stairs. He walked to the microphone and grabbed it out of her hand. Giving a laugh, Mr. Blackstone put a hand in the air as if to silence the crowd. "Now, now. Let's everyone settle down." He turned to Marley and grinned.

Marley thought steam might shoot out of his ears like a cartoon character, but she had to give him credit; the smile never faltered from his lips.

Addressing the crowd once again, his voice thickened, "Ladies and gentlemen, there's been a huge misunderstanding. I would never ask someone to do something they didn't want to do--especially not make a decision about their future over a little speck of salt."

The audience remained silent.

He glanced at Marley while he talked, "I think I speak for the town when I say that if you wanted to return home, we'd all welcome you...with open arms," he nearly choked on the last words as he spoke them. "Of course, no one wants Benjamin Miller stripped of his title or prize money over such a minor mistake. So, please, Dr. Bakersfield, take my apology for any part in this misunderstanding. I think I speak for the town, myself, and my daughter when I say welcome home." He clasped both of Marley's hands in his and shook them.

She thought he squeezed a little tighter than necessary, but at least he'd conceded. She inched toward the microphone. "Uh, thank you, Mr. Blackstone, for the unexpected, but not unwelcomed apology. I accept and plan to stay in Blackstone Haven as a dual-board certified general and plastic surgeon and would be blessed to care for this community. I'm excited to spend more time with my mother and carry on my father's legacy. As you know," she sent a pointed stare to Mr. Blackstone, "he served not only this town and his family but his country with great honor."

Mr. Blackstone's face went pale.

Marley supposed he thought she would tell the audience about his military shortcomings. Still, her father had taught her that vengeance remained with the Lord. She didn't want Mr. Blackstone to get away with destroying Benjamin's bakery, but she wasn't on a vendetta.

"I hope I can carry that level of honor forward. I'm also thankful to return to wonderful friends," she gazed at Corkie and Mrs. Klingensmith in the crowd, and then Benjamin, "and to start a new life...with a new love." Tears sprang up, and one trickled down her cheek. "Thank you all for your time."

The townspeople burst into applause, and a few people even whistled their approval.

Marley placed the microphone in its stand and turned to send a thank you to the singer for letting her hijack the stage.

He nodded and gave her a high-five.

As the band kicked off the dancing portion of the evening, Marley exited the stage. She got to the bottom stair and found Benjamin waiting on her.

He walked up to her one slow step at a time. He wore a black suit, red dress shirt, and black tie—the perfect Valentine's Day attire.

Placing a hand on his tie, Marley smoothed it before meeting his eyes. "You look so handsome. Did I tell you that earlier?"

"No, you didn't, but I'm glad to hear it. Did you mean all of that? You're staying? You want to be with me, too?"

She nodded, dropping her eyes before looking at him again from underneath her eyelashes. "Yes. Every word of it. I love you, Benjamin. I'm sorry everything got messed up, and I'm sorry it took me this long to realize who I am and what I want. But now I know--I'm a child of God, beautifully made, and I want to live here and be with you."

He clasped her hand into both of his and dropped to one knee. Gazing up at her with his piercing blue eyes, he spoke softly, but clearly, "Marley Bakersfield, will you marry me and let me spend the rest of my life loving you and showing you how beautiful you are to me?"

Marley's pulse raced, and she thought her heart might explode from happiness. "Yes, yes, a million times, yes. Of course, I'll marry you."

He jumped up. Placing his hands upon Marley's cheeks, Benjamin tilted her face up to his. He dipped his head, stopping with his lips an inch from hers, and paused. "I love you, Marley. I'll always love you."

"I love you, Benjamin Miller."

His lips pressed against hers, gently at first. Benjamin's kisses deepened and Marley sank further into him.

Marley's knees melted, the room spun, and she never wanted the kiss to end. After several seconds, she placed a hand on his chest and leaned back, lifting her gaze to Benjamin's.

He smiled down at her and a teasing glint appeared in his eyes. "Hey, does this mean you're going to start eating the stuff I bake?"

"I love you...but I think I'll stick with coffee."

He chuckled and murmured, "I guess some things never change."

She grinned up at him. "Like how I feel about you."

"Exactly," he gave her a soft kiss, "like how I feel about you."

Epilogue

Valentine's Day, One Year Later

As Marley stood in front of the church bathroom mirror, she brushed her hair and stared at her reflection. Butterflies flitted in her stomach as she prepared for the evening. She flounced the skirt of the gown she'd selected—a snow-white confection with a billion layers of tulle and a snug bodice.

Tara stepped into the room, knocking on the doorframe. "Hey, are you ready? Don't want to be late for this." She grinned at her friend in the mirror.

"I think so. I need to slip on my shoes and touch up my lipstick. Then, I'm set. What do you think?" She grabbed the edges of her skirt, swaying it side to side. "Too much?"

Tara's eyes moistened. "I think it's perfect. You look gorgeous."

"Thanks." She glanced at herself one final time. Her scar peeked out from underneath her bangs, but today she didn't mind it. She'd learned to embrace it as part of her story. It held a reminder of her past and how far she'd come—how strong she could stand in God's love for her. She stepped into her sapphire shoes, the something blue for the day.

"Here, take this." Tara handed Marley her bouquet, tucking a handkerchief inside. "Something borrowed and something old. The dress is something new. Now you're ready."

Tears sprang to Marley's eyes, and she threw her arms around her best friend. "Thank you, Tara. Thank you for being a wonderful friend...thank you for everything. Especially helping distract Mr. Blackstone a year ago. If it hadn't been for your dazzling conversational skills, I don't know if we'd be here today."

Tara waved. "I didn't do much. Just talked his ear off." She chuckled. "Who'd have thought a year ago you'd be standing here, ready to marry Benjamin Miller on Valentine's Day?"

Marley straightened herself and dabbed away the tears. "I know. I'm so thankful to be living the life God planned for me."

"Well, let's get you down the aisle and get this part of the plan started." Tara fixed Marley's veil and smiled. "How do you feel?"

Marley cast a final glance in the mirror. "I feel beautiful." She followed her friend out of the room and down the hall.

An usher opened the door to the church sanctuary as an organ played the first notes of "The Wedding March."

She lifted her eyes, found Benjamin's, and took her first step into her future. Even though she'd come home to a place of past hurts, God had healed her heart and given her a gift greater than this wedding, greater than a fancy dress, greater than the medical practice. He'd given her His love—his unfaltering, unwavering, unconditional love. And Marley knew if she abided in it, she'd always feel...well, beautiful.

The End.

Other books in the Dose of Love series

Harte Broken
Perfectly Imperfect

About the Author

Jill writes inspirational romantic fiction with a medical theme. This novel is part of the *A Dose of Love* series. Each story can stand alone, but they all feature strong female leads facing challenging life circumstances while finding love along the way. Jill's debut novel, *Harte Broken*, was inspired by her love of romance and the experience of losing her mother on the same day of her daughter's birth. It raises the question, "What happens when the best day is also the worst one?"

Jill is a physician and mom who loves coffee, travel, and anything glittered. She treasures spending time with her husband and children, who are her heart and greatest joy.